T0162734

Creating Your Teaching Plan:
A Guide for
Effective Teaching

Arleen P. Mariotti
University of South Florida

authorHOUSE®

AuthorHouse™
1663 Liberty Drive
Bloomington, IN 47403
www.authorhouse.com
Phone: 1-800-839-8640

©2009 Arleen P. Mariotti. All rights reserved.

No part of this book may be reproduced, stored in a retrieval system, or transmitted by any means without the written permission of the author.

First published by AuthorHouse 9/21/2009

ISBN: 978-1-4490-0451-4 (e)
ISBN: 978-1-4490-0450-7 (sc)

Printed in the United States of America
Bloomington, Indiana

This book is printed on acid-free paper.

Preface

Creating Your Teaching Plan: A Guide for Effective Teaching was written to provide you with numerous practical, research-based ideas which you can use in your particular classroom setting. It contains tried and tested strategies to help you be successful, whether you're a new teacher, one returning after an absence, or an experienced teacher looking for new ideas.

After working for years as a teacher and mentor to new teachers, I saw that many of them needed assistance in developing a plan to help them start their year in a manner that would increase the likelihood of their success. Some new teachers think that if they have a set of classroom rules posted, a few interesting lesson ideas, and a love of children, the rest will fall into place. Unfortunately, research on effective teaching tells us otherwise.

This worktext is organized around five critical areas necessary for successful teaching:
- Starting the Year
- Planning
- Monitoring and Assessing Learning
- Managing the Classroom
- Enhancing Reading/Literacy Skills

Specifically, you will examine strategies for effective questioning, responding, and praise, giving students voice, incorporating active learning, and developing a warm and inviting classroom climate.

After you have completed the activities in this worktext, you will have a written plan for starting your year. This is not a guarantee that the year will be easy or successful, but you will have developed the foundation necessary to enhance student learning.

Good luck.

Acknowledgements

Many thanks to all the teachers who provided ideas and inspiration for this worktext and to those who gave assistance in its preparation. A special thanks to Gayla Snyder who edited and gave support to the project.

Contents

Chapter 4: Monitoring Learning and Adjusting Instruction   51

Chapter 5: Assessing Learning   63

Chapter 6: Classroom Management: Focusing on Prevention   83

Chapter 7: Classroom Management: Communicating Expectations   97

Chapter 8: Enhancing Students' Reading Comprehension   115

References   139

A good teacher is like a candle-
it consumes itself to light
the way for others.-Author Unknown

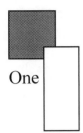

One

Starting Off Right

Remember your first day of school? The night before you probably couldn't sleep thinking about what was to come. You wondered who your teachers would be, which of your friends would be in your class, if you would know anyone, if you would get lost, and a thousand other things. Try to remember how exciting and frightening the first days were as, now, you plan to meet your students.

Perhaps nothing is as important to the school year as what happens in your classroom the first few days and weeks of school. During this time, you will establish three crucial aspects of your classroom: expectations for learning and behavior, a positive learning environment, and your relationship with your students.

Research supports the fact that effective teachers at all levels begin their year with systematic and orderly instruction in rules, procedures and routines. In fact, Buckley and Cooper (1978) found that effectively teachers had developed clearly established routines in the first week of school. Marzano (2003) summarized the research saying the beginning of the year is the "linchpin for effective classroom management."   The start of any year and/or grading period is the time for you to establish who you are, what you expect, and how you expect everyone in your classroom will behave and be treated.

Creating your Classroom

Think about places you enjoy visiting—a restaurant, retail store, or business. Do you like going to these places because you're made to feel comfortable or safe? Think about this for a minute…sometimes a favorite place isn't expensive or fancy, but a place where people smile and recognize you (they don't have to know your name). Everyone is pleasant, the place is clean and "homey," the surroundings are pleasing to the eye and easy on the emotions. If this place is a restaurant, the food is good and plentiful and every time you go, the food is <u>always</u> good and plentiful. The servers

> The beginning is the most important part of the work. - Plato

attend to you by always checking to see if you need anything. (Do you agree that there's nothing worse than getting your food and then never seeing the server again until it's time for the bill?) We could go on but you get the point. Your favorite places create positive memories for you.

Building on our analogy above, if you want students to come to your class ready and eager to learn, you must provide a climate that invites them to come back everyday. The "food"

1

is your lesson. The service is how you respond to students and monitor their progress. Does your favorite place provide for your special needs by customizing your order? Now think about your students. Does one lesson, served in the same manner, suit all of your students? Of course not! Just like that small business, everything you do sets the tone or climate of your classroom and developing that climate begins on the first day of school. You must set out to create a wonderful memory for every student in your classroom.

Meeting Your Students

In Harry Wong's *First Days of School* (2001), he says we need to consider students' seven questions for the first day and plan accordingly:

Am I in the right room?	What are the rules?
Where do I sit?	Who is the teacher as a person?
How will I be graded?	Will the teacher treat me as a human being?
What will I learn this year?	

Let's consider how these seven questions establish your climate, expectations and student relationships.

Am I in the right room?
Where do I sit?

One the first day, welcome students to your classroom by standing at the door, smiling, and checking their registration card or their name against your roster. Have a readable and visible sign outside your door with your name, room number, grade level or subject (or both). Some teachers post their rosters so students can check for their name.

It's important to give each child directions for finding his/her seat. Depending on the age of the students, you might have assigned seating by placing nameplates on the desk or a seating chart posted on the board. Young children may need to be escorted to a seat. Another technique is to give students a card upon entering and they have to find the matching card on a desk. For example, an English teacher might hand students a part of speech card (noun, verb, etc.) and they have to find a desk with a word that matched (pencil, talk). A math teacher can give students an equation card as they enter and they have to find the desk with the answer. An intermediate teacher might cut playing cards in half and students have to find their matching half. Whatever method you choose, it is unwise to allow students to mill about or run around the room. This is your first "test" in developing a procedure for entering the room and creating a positive work environment.

You need to orient students to your classroom. Show them where work is turned in, the location of centers and/or computer stations, where textbooks and resource materials are kept, etc. If they don't have a map of the school, provide one. Make sure they know how to get to key places from your room, like the media center, nearest restroom, and the clinic.

Another key to establishing your work environment is to post an assignment. Tell students to begin work immediately upon finding their seat. This first activity should be presented as bellwork (sometimes called Do Nows) and one that is easy to complete- a word search, a short writing prompt, a coloring sheet, a review handout, an interest inventory or an information sheet. You should also have the day's agenda and assignments written in an easy-to-see location. (This also cuts down on the *What are we going to do today?* questions.) These techniques establish how you expect your students to enter the room and begin class.

Activity

1.1 Design a poster or some type of sign to designate your room, your name and any other pertinent information for the first day of school.

1.2 Create a method for your students to find their seat for the first day of school.

Who is the teacher as a person?
How will I be graded?
What will I learn this year?

In addition to the administrative tasks of checking the roll, etc., you should plan your "introductory speech." In your brief talk, explain what they will learn in your class. You can give students a glimpse at the planned projects, field trips and special events by presenting a power point of last year's activities or posting student work from a previous year. Are you a new teacher? Don't fret. Just tell them what they will be doing. Secondary teachers might develop a written syllabus that also outlines how students will be graded. One of the most important pieces of information to give students at this time is a materials list. They should know from the onset what materials they will need to be successful in your classroom and a date by which you expect them to have those materials.

Expect the unexpected in the first week of school. Be over-prepared but be really flexible. too.

If students do not bring pencil and paper on the first day, provide a loaner and tell them you expect them to be prepared in the future. At some point during your first days of school, you should have a class discussion on what the phrase *ready for class* means and write their ideas on a poster. Some teachers ask students to list the tools necessary in different jobs, i.e., plumber, carpenter, doctor, student, and then discuss how they would regard a person who showed up to do a job without their tools. Finally, ask students how teachers might view students who do not show up with their tools. While this might seem "elementary," you'd be surprised at the number of secondary students who come to school unprepared. Informing students of your expectations on preparedness avoids the *"I didn't know"* response.

Let's pause for a moment and reflect on our business analogy. If you were a new hire, your boss would tell you what was expected of you, where to put your "things," what to do when you came in to work (sign-in, punch a time clock, etc.), and possibly give you a quick tour of the place. Shouldn't you, the teacher, do the same with your new students?

What are the rules?

During the first few days, people often say it's a "honeymoon" period, that is, students and teachers are really nice to each other. Actually, students are sizing you up. The research supports the use of rules and procedures, their explanation, and even the demonstration of the rules to the students. Your classroom rules should be established, posted and discussed on the first day of school. Here are some examples:

> Be on time.
> Bring your materials to class everyday.
> Listen to the speaker.
> Keep your hands and feet to yourself.
> Avoid negative comments toward others.

Classroom rules and procedures will vary from teacher to teacher and some teachers prefer to have students develop the rules and a classroom contract. Whether you create your own set of rules or invite student input, you should discuss with students what would happen in any work place that did not have rules. For example, ask students, *What might happen if there weren't any work rules at a hospital, restaurant, or department store?* Students will surprise you and provide a whole list of possible consequences. Experienced teachers all agree--a set of guidelines for creating a pleasant work environment is absolutely necessary.

Post your rules and go over them as part of your classroom "tour." If you plan to have student input into the development of classroom rules, indicate that the posted rules are in effect until the class can establish their own set. If you develop a syllabus, include the rules in it. It's advisable to have students take home the syllabus and have their parents sign it. This can serve as students' first "homework" assignment and shows your students and their parents you value a safe working environment.

1.2 Develop 3-5 classroom rules and a method to teach the rules during the first days of school.

List of Rules:	How to Teach Rule:

Will the teacher treat me as a human being?

Okay, let's return to our favorite business. How do the people treat you when you walk in the door? Do they smile or frown? Do they say *Hello* or do they act inconvenienced? Do they send you off with a *Have a nice day* or do they sign and act pleased that you're leaving? Think about these things as we examine some of the steps you might take in creating a positive climate in your classroom.

Greet students. Learn their names. Say *Please* and *Thank you*. Smile. Forget the old adage: *Don't smile until November*. "A smile is the most effective way to create a positive climate, to disarm an angry person, and to convey the message: *Do not be afraid of me; I am here to help you.* " (Wong, pg. 73).

> Students should feel as though you really like them. Make eye contact and be interested in what they say (even if you're not!) –Lois, veteran teacher.

Think now about how the people in your favorite business look. Are they neat and clean or are they untidy? Are their clothes pressed or wrinkled? Do they look professional and appropriate or are they wearing old T-shirts and torn jeans? Students' first impression of you develops before you open your mouth to speak. You should dress to separate yourself from your students. One way to gain respect is to dress appropriately for work. Always come to work in clean, neat and ironed clothes. It says to students that you care enough about yourself to look good and it says you care about your students to look good for them.

Your first words are equally important. Once students have found their seats and have begun the bellwork, you need to stand in front of the class and welcome them. Do not sit or stand behind your desk. Desks and podiums are a barrier between them and you. Begin your introductory speech by introducing yourself: *Good morning. I'm Mrs. Smith. I am your teacher for this year. I want to thank you for coming into the room quietly and finding your seat so quickly. I would like to tell you some of the things we will be learning about in this class.* Is this is your first year of teaching? Well...don't tell them! Tell them where you went to college and some of the jobs you've had. Tell them how thrilled you are that they are in your class. What about personal stuff, like married, single, or kids? Leave that information at home. In the first weeks of school, your goal is to establish yourself as a competent, credible, and knowledgeable teacher.

You should also communicate in your opening speech, positive expectations. An expectation is what you believe will or will not happen (Wong, 2001). Research confirms that students' level of learning is related to their teacher's expectations. One of the easiest ways to communicate positive expectations is in your verbal exchanges with students. Here are some phrases to try out:

In my classroom everyone can achieve who tries.
If you participate and try you will learn.
Each one of you can do the work in this class.

Activity

1.4 Write your opening speech to your students.

The first days of a school year can be tough for everyone. For some children, their first day in your classroom will occur in October or January or even April. These late-entry students will have the same concerns as those who arrived in August and you'll need a plan to orient them to your classroom.

First Day Procedures

Your students should be introduced to a few procedures during the first day of school. This is an important aspect of classroom management.
A procedure is the way something is done. The first procedure to teach your students is how to enter the room and begin work. If you stand at the door and greet them as they enter, you send an important message. By the end of your first day, you also should have taught the procedure for exiting the room. <u>Never</u> allow students to leave your room because a bell rang. Remember, <u>you</u> dismiss the class, not the bell. To accomplish this, stop whatever you are doing five minutes before the end of class. Review with the students how you will dismiss them and what behavior is expected. It might go like this: *Class, thank you for your attention. It's been a busy first day. In a few minutes, you will be leaving to go to _____. I will call you by row (table, etc) to leave. I expect you to gather all your materials and belongings now and, when called, you will calmly walk out through the exit*

> Entering the Room
>
> 1. Walk into the room.
> 2. Sit in your assigned seat.
> 3. Sharpen your pencil before the tardy bell.
> 4. Begin your bellwork promptly.

door. By controlling this procedure the very first day and every day afterward, you have established the tone of your classroom as an orderly work environment. It's also a good idea to have your procedures written on chart paper or on the board for the first week of school.

What if students do not follow the procedure? Do <u>not</u> ignore it. Talk quietly to the student(s) and communicate that you expect students in your classroom to act in a certain manner. Remember to praise the students when they do follow your procedures.

There are many procedures that include a bell, such as fire drills, bomb threats, tornado drills, etc. You do not need to teach these on the first day, however, your behavior would be the same. You control the students' exit, not the bell.

Getting Their Attention-The Quiet Signal

Another procedure to teach students on the first day of school is how you will get their attention. If someone isn't paying attention they will not learn what you want them to learn. For this reason, on day one you should establish how you will ask students to stop and listen. You could ring a small bell, play a chime, or blow a whistle. Some teachers clap their hands three times and others use a hand signal. Whatever you choose, you will need to teach this signal to students and practice it during the first day of school.

A very easy way to practice the quiet signal is to teach it with an activity. For example, introduce your signal. Then instruct students to tell their partner their name and how they spent their summer. In the middle of this sharing, use your quiet signal. Thank students who responded appropriately. Then continue the sharing activity (or any activity you've devised for this purpose.) Use the quiet signal again when you wish to stop the activity. Another way to introduce your quiet signal is to engage students in some content-related activity and use the signal when you want them to stop. There are many ways to teach the signal. The important thing is to introduce it on day one and practice it every day thereafter.

This is probably common sense, but *don't* pair your quiet signal with yelling or statements such as, *Okay, get quiet NOW. Come on, guys. Listen up!* Give your signal and wait—patiently—until all students' eyes are on you and all talking has ceased. Thank the students who attended to the signal and continue with your lesson.

Activity

1.5 Here are some procedures you will need the first week of school with room to add your own. Create a plan for teaching your procedures.

Procedure	When Introduced	How Introduced
Entering the Room		
Exiting the Room		
Quiet Signal		

Activity

1.6 Brainstorm ways you can meet the seven questions students have on the first day of school and write them in the chart below.

Question	Possible Ways to Answer the Question
Am I in the right class?	
Where do I sit?	
Who is the teacher?	
What are the rules?	
What will I learn?	
How will I be evaluated?	
Does the teacher care?	

Ice Breakers

One way to establish the climate of your classroom is to conduct an icebreaker activity during the first few days of school. These activities help you get to know something about your students and give your students an opportunity to meet new people. It's sad when, after several months of school, students do not know the names of their classmates. Students work together better and communicate in more positive ways when they know each other. Here are some easy, quick and adaptable ice breakers you can try:

Group Sequence
Divide the class into groups of 3 or 4 and provide each member with a part of a sequence, i.e. comic strip, recipe, lab experiment, news story, pictures from a picture book. Instruct the students to work together to find the correct sequence.

ABC Acrostic
Tell students to write the letters of their first and last name (or just their first) down the side of their paper and then write words, or a sentence, starting with those letters to describe themselves. For example, Ann might write *able, nice, nature-lover.* They share these with a partner or small group.

Favorite T-Shirt
Give students a paper outline of a t-shirt and ask them to design a t-shirt that says something about them. Have them share it with the class.

M&Ms, Goldfish, or TP share
Pass a bowl filled with M&Ms or Goldfish or a roll of toilet paper. Ask students to take as many as they want from the bowl but caution them not to eat YET (the M&Ms or Goldfish). Students then have to reveal a number of things about themselves to the class that correspond to the number of candies, goldfish or TP sheets they took.

Wanted Posters
Explain that everyone will be introducing themselves to others through "Wanted Posters" which they will create themselves. Show a sample "Wanted Poster" and give everyone paper, and a pencil, or marker. Allow 5-10 minutes for everyone to complete their posters. Then tell everyone to circulate around reading each other's posters and sharing their own. Allow sufficient time for all the students to read each other's posters and then call the group back to sit in their seats. There are many ice breaker activities listed on the Internet and your veteran colleagues may have a suggestion or two, as well. It's a good idea to have a few of these ready to use during the first few weeks.

The First Academic Assignment

It is clear that your classroom is a place of business and the business of your classroom is learning. But how do you must communicate that message daily to students? During the first days you need to provide academic tasks on which all students can feel success. Usually, you will not be distributing textbooks or workbooks in the first days. Hence, you will need to think about content-related activities that are can be completed without the aid of a textbook. Here are some examples:

> teacher read-aloud,
> journal writing,
> vocabulary puzzles,
> word searches,
> editing activities,
> discussing current events/newspaper story,
> review of last-year's content.

Pre-test? Try to avoid this on the first day. Students with a history of failure may experience failure yet again on a test before the class content actually starts. Those with limited prior knowledge may feel they will not succeed because they don't know anything. To prevent sending the "failure" message instead of your "expectations for success" message, avoid pre-tests in the first few days of school-even if they don't count toward the student's grade.

> The important thing is not so much that every child should be taught, as that every child should be given the wish to learn. –John Lubbock

Academic tasks are a perfect means for you to teach procedures, such as, how to head the paper, how to turn in papers, and what to do if you finish early. Use these opportunities in the first days to teach and reinforce your classroom procedures.

Here are some examples of content-related tasks appropriate for intermediate students and higher that can be adapted for a variety of age/grade levels:

Students write the alphabet down the long side of their notebook paper. They then write a word or phrase that they know about the subject that begins with each letter. For example, in a science class, they might write "aerobic" for A, "biome" for B, etc. Encourage students to try to write something for each letter. After a predetermined time limit, divide the class into small groups to add words beside the letters that they do not already have written on the paper. At this point, you may have groups share their responses for those hard letters and you may even want to award a prize to the group (or student) who has the most words.

Students write the answer to the question: *What are the tools of a _____* (scientist, mathematician, geographer, writer, etc.) The class discusses their answers and the teacher may fill-in some gaps. Then students draw a picture of a _____ (scientist, mathematician, geographer, writer, etc.) and the class discusses why they choose to draw the person in that manner. This lesson can be a cooperative group project.

Students write ten adjectives to describe their summer. They either use those adjectives as part of a get-to-know you activity in orally describing their summer or write a letter to you introducing themselves and what they did during their vacation. (This lesson can be used after any holiday break.)

Students read a content-related article from a magazine or newspaper and react to teacher-prepared questions in small groups followed by a whole class discussion.

If you need content ideas for the beginning of the year, search the Internet. Here are some sites to get you started:

www.atozteacherstuff.com   www.school.discovery.com
www.edhelper.com   www.teachersdesk.org

Don't forget to ask your experienced colleagues for ideas, too.

Activity

1.7 Develop three academic tasks that all your students can successfully complete without a text for the first week of school.

Other Critical Considerations for the Beginning of the Year

Before you meet your students there are some other decisions you must make. These include:

- How will your students keep their work-- In a 3-ring binder with dividers, in folders, in a portfolio?
- How will the notebook/folder be organized?
- Will you have a predetermined homework schedule? What is your homework policy?
- How will you collect homework and classwork assignments? How will papers be distributed?
- How will you notify parents of the homework assignments?
- How will students be graded-academically and for behavior/conduct?
- Will you accept late work?
- How will you get work to absent students?
- What will the classroom physically look like? How will desks/seats be arranged? Where will materials be located?
- Will there be learning centers? How will they be used? How will children work through these centers?
- Will you have computers and what will be the procedure for student use?

- Where will your desk be located?

What YOU need to know before the first day

Here are some things you should find out before you meet your first student.

- ✓ Schedules: What are the daily bell schedule(s), lunch times, conference/planning time, time to report to work, and time to leave work?
- ✓ Duties: Do you have assigned duties during the day?
- ✓ Lunch: Where do faculty eat? Is the cafeteria food any good?

What are the procedures and policies for:

- ➢ Taking students to lunch
- ➢ Marking student attendance and tardies
- ➢ Finding a substitute if you're sick or have an emergency
- ➢ Fire drills, bomb threats, tornados, etc.
- ➢ Handling a student illness or emergency
- ➢ Handling a fight
- ➢ Making copies
- ➢ Purchasing equipment and classroom supplies
- ➢ Grading students

Preplanning Time

In a perfect education world, you would be hired with enough time to learn your curriculum, prepare your classroom for students, and develop a few fascinating lessons. You would have enough materials and textbooks for all your students and your classroom would be equipped with all the modern technology you could imagine.

But we don't have a perfect education world. You might be hired the day before children report to school. You may find that you are hired for one grade level only to be transferred to a different one when the school year begins. Even worse you may lose your position at the school due to low student enrollment and be transferred to another school site.

New teachers frequently say they were not prepared for the amount of paperwork during the first weeks of school and, because they were required to attend numerous meetings during preplanning, they did not have time to adequately get their room ready for children. You need to focus whatever time you have during preplanning on getting to know your curriculum and materials, developing your management plan, and developing lessons for the first week to capture your students' interests.

Getting your room ready means your room should be clean and inviting but it doesn't have to be perfect. Keep to the basics:
1. arrange student desks/chairs so they are facing forward and all eyes are on you.
2. place your desk so you can monitor your students if you're sitting there
3. plan your lessons and organize all your materials for the first week of school
4. ensure all your AV and technological equipment works properly
5. make and display your rules and procedures for the first week in a prominent place
6. prepare a welcome sign and one bulletin board

There's certainly a lot to consider as you prepare for your first day of teaching. But the most important thing to remember is that you want to create a positive memory that your students will talk about with their friends and family. Some years ago my stepson came home from his first day of school and, when asked the proverbial, *"How was your first day?"* he answered with *"I heard a lot of rules."* Wouldn't you rather create an atmosphere where each student enjoyed the time in your class, experienced success, and felt noticed by YOU?

Activity

1.8 Develop your plan for the first day of school. Be sure to address the seven questions proposed by Wong.

Activity	Time Allotment	Description
Student Welcome		
Bellwork		
Get-to-Know You Activity		
Presentation of Rules		
Content Activity(ies)		
Filler (Sponge) Activities, i.e. word searches, crossword puzzles		

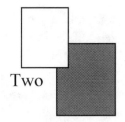

Two

When planning for a year, plant corn. When planning for a decade, plant trees. When planning for life, train and educate people.
-Chinese Proverb

Planning for Effective Instruction

All professionals plan: surgeons plan an operation, coaches plan for the game, generals plan battles, actors and directors plan a scene, and lawyers plan a case. Instructional planning is the essence of good teaching.   Effective teachers plan; they do not teach "off the cuff." They plan for the year, the grading period, the month, the week and the day. Generally, teachers who prepare lesson plans, follow their plans and focus more closely on content objectives. When you engage in effective instructional planning you will be more organized, have minimal student misbehaviors, and increase your confidence in the classroom.

Lesson planning requires that you use your "teacher brain." That is, you need to ask questions before you present content to students. As you examine your curriculum, or scope and sequence, ask the following:

What information and/or skills need to be taught?
What prerequisite knowledge and/or skills do students need to have?
Why am I teaching this?
How will students demonstrate they understand or can perform the new learning?
What's the best way for me to present this?
How can I incorporate active learning?
How can I make this interesting?
What materials will I use?
What is the best way to distribute the materials?
If I'm using groups, how should I group my students?
What might give my students the greatest difficulty?
What could possibly go wrong?

Long-Term Planning

One of the beauties of teaching is that every year is a new beginning. It also means teachers must engage in extensive long-term planning.   Long-term planning includes:
1. examining the standards and learning objectives for your course(s)
2. breaking up the content objectives and units into grading periods (6-week, 9-weeks, etc.)
3. scheduling units, projects and content into monthly and weekly time periods.

The essential learning topics and/or objectives are usually found in your curriculum guide(s), typically developed by your district. Standards lead to objectives and subject area topics lead to units.

> He who dares to teach must never cease to learn.-Anonymous

Learning objectives and topics are usually given to you in the form of a curriculum guide, or scope and sequence. This is your starting point. You may add supplementary objectives and topics to the list, but it is generally a good idea to stick to the curriculum in your first year. Some curriculum guides are very explicit by indicating page numbers and dates for instruction. Other guides are merely a list of topics. Some content areas may not have any curriculum guide and you must supply the learning objectives and topics. If this is the case, try some research on the Internet. Often, you will locate prepared guides for your subject area.

Imagine you have a curriculum guide with just a list of topics. The first thing to do is to talk with your department head (r subject area leader), or grade level leader. Ask for advice. Experienced teachers love to provide their expertise and guidance. Ask what they cover at the beginning of the year and how they use their textbook(s) and workbook(s). This may sound crazy, but a novice teacher once asked in December, *You mean you actually use the textbook?*

Experienced teachers usually develop written plans for the course, the grading period (term), the unit, the week and the day. Look at the planning illustration below (Burden & Byrd, 2007):

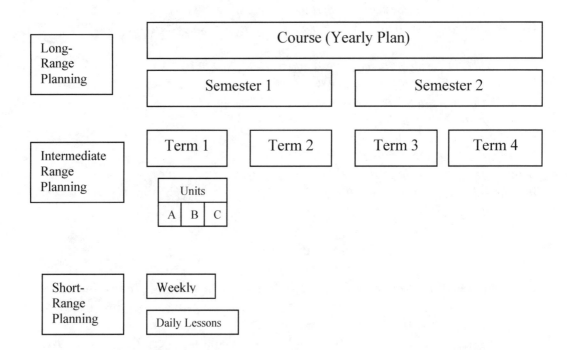

Course planning involves organizing and scheduling the content you're going to teach. Here are some examples of long-range course planning that cover two grading periods. Notice that these broad plans are focused on units (topics) and skills rather than specific learning objectives.

Reading

<table>
<tr><td>

__Term 1__

Introduce story elements
Reading Skills: asking questions
                   main idea
                   context clues
                   predicting
                   cause and effect

Units: Folk Tales
                 The short story
Projects: Anthology of Folk Tales
                 Write a short story

Materials: Text
                 Library books-folk tales

</td><td>

__Term 2__

Continue story elements
Reading Skills: inferencing
                   comparison-contrast
                   sequencing
                   text structures

Units: Novel study
                 Mythology
Projects: Create a brochure on a novel
                 Research a mythological
                 character
Materials: Text
                 Class set of novel
                 Internet

</td></tr>
</table>

Science

<table>
<tr><td>

__Term 1__

Unit: Scientific Method
Skill: Metric Measurement
Unit: Environmental Science:
                 Ecosystems
                 Habitat
                 Interactions
                 Energy flow
                 Environmental issues
Projects: Biome Study
                 Poster of scientific method
Materials: Text
                 Science Videos
                 Lab Equipment

</td><td>

__Term 2__

Unit: Continue scientific method
Unit: The cell
                 6 Kingdoms:
                  archebacteria
                  eubacteria
                  fungi
                  protists
                  plants and animals
Projects: Create model of cell
                 Develop pamphlet of 6 kingdoms
Materials: Text
                 Science Videos
                 Lab Equipment
                 Library books/Internet

</td></tr>
</table>

Mathematics

<table>
<tr><td>

__Term 1__

Units: Data organization and analysis
         Probability
         Fractions and Decimals

Projects: Create survey, organize
            and analyze data
Materials: Text and workbook
         Manipulatives
         Probability games

</td><td>

__Term 2__

Units: Rate and Ratio
         Integers
         One Step Equations

Projects: Comparison shopping

Materials: Text and workbook
         Newspapers

</td></tr>
</table>

You're probably thinking that these plans aren't very specific. In fact, you might be wondering, "What do I teach about *data organization and analysis*?" Good for you. Long range planning is BROAD. Specifics come later. If planning for 10 months sccm too daunting a task, then plan just the first term. It is crucial for you to think beyond the day or the week as you begin planning.

2.1 Get a copy of your school district's curriculum guide, scope and sequence, and/or textbook and
1. develop a long-term course plan covering 2 grading periods for a subject area
2. include possible projects for each term

Term ___	Term ___
Units	Units:
Possible Projects:	Possible Projects:
Materials List	Materials List

Weekly and Daily Lesson Planning

Once you have developed your long-range plan, you can focus on your weekly and daily plans. Interestingly, effective teachers do not use one model for planning (Shavelson, 1987) and most of their planning is not committed to paper but remains a mental process (Clark and Yinger, 1979). However, until you become comfortable with the instructional objectives and teaching materials, it is highly recommended that you develop written plans. These plans may be detailed notes, an outline, or a list of "things" to cover. Whatever its form, written plans will provide you with direction and develop your sense of security in the classroom.

Daily lesson planning begins by looking at your week and determining the learning objectives to be covered. It's a good idea to invest in a Teacher's Plan Book or a calendar/date book with large blocks to write your plans. You will want to include any school events or activities that will impact your teaching time. Be sure to write your plans

IN PENCIL. The reason? The teaching day is fraught with interruptions, such as, fire drills, announcements and visitors. You will also find that what you thought would take 10 minutes, took your students 45 minutes and visa versa. Situations such as these will require you to adjust your teaching plans on a regular basis.

Objectives

Let's begin with the learning objective. An objective describes what students should know or be able to do as a result of the lesson. Here are some examples:

Students will define the following words…
Students will write a complete declarative sentence.
Students will compare and contrast urban and rural life.
Students will illustrate the water cycle.

Do you see a pattern? First, the verb in the objective is something we can see students do. Practically speaking, if students can't do what the objective says, they haven't learned. Second, each objective is a single sentence and extremely focused. Lastly, the objective is clearly written so that everyone understands it, even your students.

Sometimes, objectives contain a standard, or the level of performance that is desirable. Consider the following behavioral objective:

Given a blank map of Asia, the student will be able to identify 90% of the countries located in the area.

This example describes the observable behavior (identifying the countries), the conditions (given a blank map of Asia), and the standard (90%).

Today, learning objectives may disregard the conditions and standards. What is always included, however, is the most important aspect of the objective - a written indicator of the behavior using measurable or observable verbs.

There are many lists of objective verbs (define, write, compare, illustrate, etc). A common list of objectives is that of Benjamin Bloom(1956). In the following chart, Bloom's taxonomy of cognitive thinking provides us a way to organize and create learning objectives.

Objectives by Bloom's Cognitive Level

Level	What is required of the learner	Verbs	Example
Knowledge	Recall, recognize or identify previously learned material	List, label, name, state, define, find, locate, tell, match, state	The student will list 3 major cities in France.
Understanding (Comprehension)	Translates, explains, or interprets prior learning	Describe, give an example, explain, summarize, interpret, paraphrase, restate, retell	The student will explain in words the procedure for solving one-step equations.
Application	Selects, transfers and uses information to solve a new problem	Use, solve, propose, apply, compute, demonstrate, draw, show	The student will write 3 compound sentences in a paragraph.
Analysis	Examines and take apart new information.	Examine, categorize, compare and contrast, simplify, classify, diagnose, diagram, distinguish	The student will compare and contrast vertebrate and invertebrate animals.
Synthesis	Creates a new product, plan or proposal	Create, design, invent, compose, plan, produce, predict	The student will create an original poem.
Evaluation	Assesses, criticizes or appraises using a standard or criteria	Judge, recommend, criticize, evaluate, justify, defend, rank, rate, support	The student will evaluate a list of ideas on the solution to global warming.

The important thing to remember is that we do not teach a TOPIC; we teach to an OBJECTIVE. We do not teach the American Civil War; we teach children to identify the causes and effects of the Civil War. We do not teach about the environment; we teach children to distinguish between niche, habitat, and ecosystem. Effective teachers know the goals of their instruction. If asked, *"What are you teaching?"* effective teachers respond with their objective, *"I am teaching students to solve one-step equations."*

Where do you find objectives? Most of the time objectives are provided in the form of curriculum guides, or the scope and sequence, for your subject area(s). You also might locate objectives in your teaching materials, textbooks, or in professional publications.

Here's another good question: How many objectives should guide the lesson? Remember that a lesson plan covers the allocated time for one period which may be 60, 90 or 120 minutes. Allocated time begins the moment a student enters your classroom until the dismissal bell, or, in elementary school, from the moment a new subject begins through the transition to the next subject. The allocated time is the total time given for teacher instruction and student learning and a lesson plan should cover all allocated minutes.

Take a look at this example:

Unit: Health
Topic: Respiratory System
Objectives: The student will
                   Explain the function of the respiratory system
                   Name the organs involved in the respiratory system
                   Diagram the path of air in the human respiratory system
                   Define the terms breathing and respiration
                   Explain the process of gas exchange

If your allocated time was 120 minutes, you *might* be able to achieve all of the objectives listed above. But if your allocated time was 60 minutes, there's no way you would get to all of them. Clearly, one factor in your selection of objectives is allocated time.

How do students demonstrate their learning?

Now that you know what to teach, you need to decide how your students will demonstrate that they reached your learning objective. In addition to the "traditional" measures of quizzes, tests, and classroom Q & A, there are many alternative assessment methods that allow students to show you what they've learn. In the book, *Instruction for All Students*, by Paula Rutherford (2007), there is an extensive list of products from which you may choose. For example, students might dramatize, create a documentary, write an editorial or letter, create a brochure or travel log, make a flip chart, or develop a checklist.

Rather than creating the assessment piece as your last step in lesson planning, think about it first. Wiggins and McTighe (1998) label this the *backward design process.* They maintain that instead of starting with the textbook and favorite activities (as many teachers do), we must begin by thinking about the evidence we need to collect to document that the desired learning goal has been achieved. To accomplish this, we cannot use assessment as an afterthought or because it comes at a good time. We must consider upfront how we will design our assessments and collect our data. Both you and your students need to know if the learning was successful, and your objectives help identify the means to make that determination.

What are the means to reaching objectives?

Once you have the learning objective(s) and assessment products/methods, you can brainstorm activities that meet the objectives and select and sequence the appropriate activities for your students. There are many activities that can help students reach an objective so don't limit your thinking. This is also another good time to talk to experienced teacher about what they've tried and what worked for them.

Using the previous respiratory lesson as an example possible activities might include:
- Read chapter in textbook
- View video/DVD
- Lab testing carbon dioxide in exhaled air
- Draw path of oxygen and carbon dioxide in human body
- Vocabulary crossword on terms from chapter
- Brainstorm what they know about the respiratory system (KWL[*])
- Make model of how breathing takes place
- Complete study guides
- Cooperative group computer research on respiratory system (jigsaw)

You might not be able to use all of these activities. In fact, if the allocated time is 60 minutes, the first day you might only be able to brainstorm with KWL, view a video/DVD, and have students use study guide notes with the video. As you begin planning, remember: a lesson plan does not cover three days or a week. It only covers the allocated time for each day.

Now that you have a list of possible activities, your next step is to select and sequence them. To do that, you must know your students. That means you must have some idea of their background knowledge and skills. Do they possess the vocabulary necessary to read and comprehend the material? Can they work cooperatively? Do they have the necessary lab skills? Do they already possess a lot of information or have relatively little on the subject?

> The most effective teacher will always be biased, for the chief force in teaching is confidence and enthusiasm.-Joyce Cary

Now you're asking, *How do I find this information?* The easiest way is to question your colleagues and students. You might give a pretest, but activities such as KWL will also provide you with the necessary information. You can begin your lesson with the question, *"What do you know about _____?"* Listening to your students' responses provides you with information about their previous learning.

Why bother with students' prior knowledge? What if you designed this brilliant lesson on linear metric measurement where students were measuring various items using metric tools? After 5 minutes you discover, to your dismay, that they don't know how to read a metric ruler. You will undoubtedly have to stop the lesson to teach how to read a metric ruler or take the chance that students will learn intuitively, if at all. Let's say you want your students to read the novel: *War of the Worlds*. When you begin the discussion, you discover that their background knowledge consists of the Tom Cruise movie and they don't have any knowledge of the time period in which the original novel was written. At this point we can safely say: *Don't assume your students know what they need to know. Make sure they do.*

---

[*] KWL=What do I know, What do I want to learn, What did I learn.

The Weekly Plan

You're now ready for weekly planning. Weekly plans are absolutely essential! In your plan book, sketch out your schedule. This is a fluid plan and should be revised as needed. Here's an example:

Monday	Tuesday	Wednesday	Thursday	Friday
Introduce the 5 organs in the respiratory system	Examine: a. breathing & respiration b. function of the respiratory system	LAB to determine the presence of oxygen and carbon dioxide	Draw path of oxygen and carbon dioxide in the human body	LAB to develop model to explain how breathing takes place
Bellwork – Name 10 animals with lungs KWL-brainstorm respiratory system Bill Nye Video on Respiration ---Use study guide Discuss guide	Bellwork – Why do we need oxygen? Define respiration & breathing Read Ch. in Text Discuss (Q & A)	Bellwork – What are 2 functions of respiratory system? Lab – testing oxygen in air and carbon dioxide in expelled air	Bellwork – Why do people cough and sneeze? Diagram of path of oxygen and carbon dioxide (pairs) Make crossword or word search with vocabulary	Bellwork – Why is it hard to breathe on top of Mr. Everest? Make model of how breathing takes place – lab groups

Creating and keeping your weekly plans is an excellent documentation of your teaching and will be helpful to you as you plan next year. These written plans can be of value with absent students and in parent/student conferences. When administrators request to see your lesson plans, the weekly plan is usually what want.

> Write your plans in pencil and don't be afraid to make changes. Include in the weekly plans school scheduled events, such as assemblies and fire drills and parent/student conferences.

Activity

2.2 Examine your curriculum guide, or scope and sequence, and plan the first two weeks of instruction.

What is a lesson?

We can safely say that asking, *"What do I do third period?"* on your way to school or in the faculty workroom is not lesson planning. Rather lesson planning is a deliberate process that focuses on the content objective(s), the materials needed, the procedures to meet your objectives and the responses of your students. Think of it this way: When a plumber fixes a clogged sink, he/she plans a course of action. The plumber needs to answer the questions: What do I want to accomplish?, What tools do I need to get the job done?, and What steps should I take to get it done? You must do the same.

So what constitutes a lesson? As mentioned previously, a lesson covers the time period allocated for a subject. In elementary school, it might be the math period from 10:30 – 11:30 a.m. In middle or high school, it might be first period or first block. Usually, a daily lesson plan does not extend beyond the day's allotted time period. You might work on the same learning objective over several days but you should have a lesson plan for each day.

Daily Planning

The most detailed plan is the daily lesson plan. In general, a daily lesson plan contains the lesson objective, the materials needed for the lesson, and a step-by-step procedure. The procedure provides suggestions on how to implement the lesson plan and focuses on what the teacher and students do during the lesson. The procedure is divided into three distinct stages: the introduction, presentation, or main activity, and the closing.

By learning you will teach; by teaching you will understand.-Latin Proverb

In the **introduction**, you should focus on helping students recall what they already know about the topic, make predictions about the content, and establish a reason for them to know and be able to do what the lesson is targeting. In the **presentation** you will put forth the content, which can take many forms: lecture, discussion, demonstration, cooperative learning, etc., and in the **closing** the students summarize and process the new information.

Let's look at some examples:

Subject: Mathematics

Objective: Students will describe at least 4 ways math is used in the real world.
              Students will work cooperatively in a group to develop a collage showing
              math in the real world.
Materials: newspapers, magazines scissors, glue, markers, construction paper

Procedure:
1. Assign homework the night before to find and bring to class 4 pictures/ads/articles of math being used in the real world. Example: receipt, blank check, etc.
2. On the day of the project, place students into groups of 3 or 4.

3. The groups examine their materials, select other examples from the newspapers and magazines provided and compose the materials into a collage.
4. Groups select a title and sign their project.
5. After they have made the college, they explain their collage to the class.
6. Students write a brief summary of how math is used in the real world.

All the activities in this plan are focused on the two objectives. When the collages are completed and you hear their explanations, you will know if they understand how math is used in the real world. In this example, the objectives and the activities are aligned.

Now look at this example:

Subject: Geography

Objectives: Students will
                Identify 3 major cities of Germany.
                Identify 3 landforms in Germany.
                Identify 2 major rivers in Germany.
                Use vocabulary terms appropriately.

Procedure:
1. Bellwork – *Using your textbook atlas, find the following: capital of Germany, 2 major rivers in Germany, 2 large cities, and 3 landforms in Germany.*
2. Introduce various regions of Germany using enlarged pictures.
3. With whole class, review major vocabulary words from text.
4. With partners, students read the textbook section on Germany
5. Homework-Give each student a guided reading worksheet

The bellwork covers the first three objectives, so what's the focus of the rest of the lesson? In this plan, objectives and activities are not in synch. Note that the plan says: "*review major vocabulary*." Teacher reviewing is very different from the objective stated as: student "*using*" vocabulary terms. How will you know if students use the vocabulary appropriately unless they actually write or orally use them? Some of the activities in the above example need more clarification. For example, how will the student partners read the text? Will one student read while the other listens? Also note that the closing appears to be the assignment of homework, which is not a method of summarizing or processing. We can safely say that this geography lesson plan needs some refining.

Activity

2.3 Examine the lesson plan that follows. List 2 positive and 2 negative aspects of the plan.

Subject: U.S. History

Objectives: The student will
           Explain what life was like for immigrants in their new cities
           Illustrate how urbanization had an impact on American culture

Procedure:

Bellwork – *Define immigrant*

1. Discuss homework reading on the chapter with the whole class.
2. Break students into small groups. Have them complete a comparison/contrast chart on urban life and rural life at this time in American History focusing on inventions and factors that caused people to move into the cities.
3. After group project, individuals will do a Venn diagram on the differences and similarities of the immigrants who arrived on the west and east coasts of the U.S. highlighting discrimination, housing, and jobs.

Could you implement this plan? Here are some questions you might have asked: Do the activities meet all the objectives? Isn't there a difference between "*explaining*" and "*comparing and contrasting*?" How does the Venn diagram "illustrate" how urbanization impacted American culture, as stated in the objective? What will be the focus of the class discussion? What are the questions to be used in that discussion? What will the teacher do if the students didn't do their homework reading? How will students know if their work on the chart and Venn diagram is correct?

This history plan has some nice hands-on activities but the activities do not appear to teach to the objectives of the lesson. Be careful that the "cuteness" of an activity does not overshadow reaching the objective of the lesson.

The Structure of a Lesson Plan

Delivering a good lesson is more than just imparting information. You need to consider how you can connect with your students as you create your lesson plans. Each daily lesson can be divided into sections, such as: beginning, presentation, student response, and conclusion. Let's look closely at the beginning and ending of a lesson plan.

Introducing the lesson

Possibly the most important part of the daily lesson is its opening, or introduction. Here, you must grab your students' attention and explain why it's important for them to learn the day's lesson. The opening must be connected to the lesson objective so try to avoid irrelevant quotes or anecdotes. Effective teachers begin with an assignment, such as bellwork. Effective lesson starters include:

Pose a question
State a fact
Give a challenging problem
Post a visual
Review the previous lesson

Your bellwork can certainly accomplish all of the above and you'll want to structure it into your opening as much as possible. Another simple introduction is to state the objective of the lesson. It might sound like this: *Today we're continuing our study of the civil war by examining the Battle of Gettysburg. You will name the key people of the battle and be able to discuss the significance of the battle.* Here's another example: *We will be studying the cell and you will label a diagram of both an animal and plant cell.* In both examples, students know the objective of the lesson and what they will have to accomplish.

You will want to vary the way you start your lessons, and, certainly, you can combine techniques that you find effective.

Closing the lesson

The brain remembers best the beginning and the end of a lesson, so, remember to include a closing in every lesson. It's like a story that leaves loose ends—it doesn't feel right and leaves the reader thinking, "What...?" Your lessons should have a planned ending so your students can reflect on their learning. The closing can take different forms. For example, you might ask students a series of review questions, or to mentally summarize what they learned, or direct students to write a summary of their learning, or to tell their neighbor a key vocabulary definition. Closings should focus the learner back to the objective of the lesson. It might sound like: *Our lesson focused on solving one-step equations (or whatever the objective). Think through the steps. Let's list them.*

A teacher review is also appropriate. It might sound like: *Today we looked at _____ and how _____ occurred. Tomorrow we will examine _____. Think about what you learned today and come ready tomorrow to discuss _____.*

You might offer a question and say, *Think about that question. We'll start there tomorrow.*

An effective technique for a good closing is to provide a sentence stem for students to complete. It might be a good idea to have the stems numbered and written on a transparency or wall chart so you can refer students to them. It might look like the following:

1.   I learned...
2.   I discovered...
3.   To summarize today's lesson...
4.   I still don't understand...
5.   The most important thing to remember from today's lesson is...

A Mind Map, or Concept Mapping, is another effective method of closing a lesson and of using a pictorial organizer to develop concepts. These can be done as a whole class, in small groups, or individually. Simply choose a word or concept from the lesson and write it on the board (or overhead). Direct students to think about the important ideas in the reading/lesson/lab and develop a way to present these ideas on paper through words, pictures, and/or diagrams. Don't forget to tell them that there is no one way to complete a map!

> It is the supreme art of the teacher to awaken joy in creative expression and knowledge. –Albert Einstein

You might have students think about the lesson and write a test question, with its answer, on a 3x5 card. These can be used in a variety of ways, including: future bellwork, on a test or quiz, in a jeopardy game, or as part of a review.

A closing doesn't have to be long and involved. In order to avoid being caught unaware of the time and then having to bark out instructions to your students as they prepare to leave, stop your lesson five minutes before the end of the learning period (use a timer). In this manner, you can conduct your closing, assign homework, have students clear their work areas, and dismiss your students in an orderly fashion.

There's more to lesson planning than creating "neat" activities. Beginning and endings-don't plan lessons without them.

Reflection

After each lesson, the effective teacher evaluates what happened. You will need to ask yourself, "What worked? What didn't?" If you are lucky enough to teach the same lesson several times a day, you can make adjustments after each presentation. It is also advisable to make notes on what worked and what needed to be changed. You can put post-it notes in the margins of your textbook or lesson plan book to remind yourself next year of needed changes.

At the end of the day, you should reflect by asking,
Did my students reach the objective? Was what I taught today relevant and necessary for my students? What were the good and bad things that happened today? What would I do differently if I could start the day all over again?

Constant reflection on your teaching methods will improve your lessons and your confidence as a teacher.

Activity

2.4 Here's an example of a lesson plan for a middle-school level geography class. Consider the information presented, reflect on the lesson and list the positive aspects.

Lesson Plan

Subject: Geography   Date   Sept.

Objective: The student will: 1) name the cardinal and intermediate directions (N,S, etc.)
2) use the directions on a school map to locate places
3) use the directions to plan a route using a local map

What prior knowledge/skills do students need?
Students should know what a map is and for what it is used.
Students might know the cardinal directions (N, S, E, and W).

How will student mastery be determined? Students will write a route for a package delivery using the cardinal and intermediate directions.

Materials: School maps, local city maps with school clearly marked (One per student pair)

Teacher Actions	Student Actions
Introducing the Lesson Ask: Why do people use maps? Have you ever used a map? When? Was it helpful? What are different kinds of maps?	Students answer questions. Students give examples of different types of maps

Presenting the Lesson
Present the cardinal directions and intermediate directions.
Explain a compass rose
Group students into partners
Distribute school maps.
   Direct students to draw a compass rose on the map
   Ask questions:
   In what direction is the cafeteria from our classroom? If I wanted to go to the media center, in which direction would I travel? Etc.
 	
Distribute local maps with school location marked
   Ask:
   What direction is ____ from the school?
	Listen
	Take notes.
	
	Students draw a compass rose on the school map
	
	Students work with their partner to determine answers.
	
	Students work with their partner to determine answers.

In what direction would I travel to get to _____? Etc.	
Pretend you are with a delivery service like UPS. With your partner, develop a route from school to _____ to deliver a package. Write your route using the cardinal and intermediate directions.	Students work with their partner to develop route.
(after 5 minutes) Let's listen to some of your routes and see if you got your package to its destination. Everyone follow along as your peers read their routes. (solicit different students' responses)	Pairs read aloud their directions to the class and the class members follow along on the map.
Closing the Lesson (review or wrap up) Think about what you did today. What have you learned about using the cardinal and intermediate directions? (solicit different students' responses) Fold your maps neatly. Brian, please pick up the maps. Let's get your materials put away and ready for dismissal.	Students answer. Students follow procedure for dismissal

2.5 Plan a lesson for the beginning of the year. Write it on the following form and include your learning objective(s).

Lesson Plan

Subject: _____ Date _____

Objective: The student will _____

_____

What prior knowledge/skills do students need?

How will student mastery be determined?

Materials:

Teacher Actions	Student Actions
Introducing the Lesson	
Presenting the Lesson	
Closing the Lesson (review or wrap up)	

Resources for lesson planning

Need some ideas for lesson plans and activities? There are many websites in the Internet that provide free lesson plans. You can conduct a search for lesson plans by simply typing the key words: *lesson plans.* You can be more specific by typing key words such as *math lesson plans, teaching plate tectonics, teaching poetry, beginning of the year lesson plans.*

Here are some sites to get you started:

www.lessonplanspage.com
www.eduref.org
www.lessonplanz.com
www.theteacherscorner.net/lesson-plans
www.teachers.net/learning
www.atozteacherstuff.com
www.edhelper.com
www.school.discovery.com
www.pacificnet.net~mandel/index.html

What are Standards?

Educational standards describe the knowledge and skills students should have at certain points in their education. Standards should provide a clear definition of the desired outcomes of schooling and a way to measure if students have achieved those outcomes. . In other words, standards identify the goals of education, provide a benchmark for assessing student mastery, and suggest a method for judging teacher effectiveness.

Standards are written as general goals and may include broadly stated objectives. For example:

The student uses the reading process effectively. (Standard)

1. uses background knowledge of the subject and text structure knowledge to make complex predictions of content, purpose, and organization of the reading selection.
2. uses a variety of strategies to analyze words and text, draw conclusions, use context and word structures, and recognize organizational patterns.

If we examine the first sub-goal under the reading standard, we can see that it consists of a variety of instructional objectives. These include:

The student will

a) Apply background knowledge to make story predictions.
b) Recognize text structure in a given text.

c) Apply text structure to predict the purpose of the text.

So when individuals say, "teach to the standard," they mean look at the broad goal. Most states have developed a set of standards and objectives for the different content areas. It is your responsibility to know those standards and to determine the objectives and strategies for reaching them.

Here's another standard:

The student understands U.S. history from 1880 to the present day.

1. understands the role of physical and cultural geography in shaping events in the U.S. since 1890 (e.g. western settlement, immigration patterns, and urbanization).
2. understands ways that significant individuals and events influenced economic, social and political systems in the U.S. after 1880.
3. knows the causes and consequences of urbanization that occurred in the U.S. after 1880 (e.g. causes such as industrialization; consequences such as poor living conditions in cities and employment conditions).

Again, an examination of the first sub-goal may consist of the following objectives:

The student will:

a) define physical and cultural geography
b) create a timeline of major US events from 1890 to present.
c) given a major current event, discuss the roles of physical and cultural geography

Activity

2.6 Find the standards for your content and grade level. Think of ways you could reach these standards in the coming year.

If there aren't any standards available for your subject area, select any of the standards listed above and create instructional objectives designed to meet the standard.

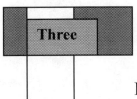

Three

Good teaching is more a
giving of right questions
than a giving of right answers.
-Josef Albers

Key Elements of Effective Lessons

Think back to a time when you were a student. What are some things teachers did that helped you learn? Do you think these strategies worked for everyone in your class? The one factor we can probably agree upon is that all students learn in different ways and, as teachers, it is our primary responsibility to see that all students have an opportunity to learn by using effective teaching strategies.

Marzano, Pickering and Pollock (2001) identified nine research based strategies that have a positive effect on student achievement. We will examine six of those strategies:

> Bellwork/Warmups
> Spaced review
> Active learning
> Nonlinguistic representations
> Learning styles
> Questioning

I.   Bellwork or Warmups

As part of the procedure for entering the room or transitioning to another subject, effective teachers usually have an assignment for students to work on that does not require teacher assistance. The activity can take many forms but should get students to focus on the content. Bellwork is short- no more than 7-8 minutes. Students should find it in the same place everyday-on the board, overhead, etc. It is also important that students know they will be accountable for completing the activity.

Here are a few examples of bellwork:

Review question(s) on previous learning or on homework
> *List 3 important facts from last night's reading*
> *Write 2 true statements and 1 false statement from Ch. 3*
> *Develop a multiple-choice question from the chapter*
> *Solve the following: 2x + 3 = 12*

Vocabulary work
> *Make a list of words with the suffix –ly*
> *Write one sentence using the following three words: seasick, sailboat, voyage*
> *Define _____*

Activating prior knowledge
> *Write 3 facts about the solar system.*
> *What do you know about _____?*
> *Write 5 examples of mixed fractions.*

Brainstorming
> *List at least 5 tools of the scientist*
> *Recall and list at least 10 landforms that are located in Africa.*

Grammar activities
> *Put ending punctuation on the sentences below:*
> *What's wrong with this sentence? Make the corrections.*
> *Write 3 declarative sentences with correct punctuation.*
> *Edit the following:*

Writing/Journal writing
> *Respond to this quote by Albert Einstein: "Anyone who has never made a mistake has never tried anything new."*
> *Write a paragraph using these words: lunchroom, lizard, potato chips, and hair extensions*
> *Have you ever lost something important to you? Describe how you felt.*

Notice that the examples above should not require teacher assistance and each can be completed within a 5-8 minute timeframe. Here are some suggestions to increase the probability of student success on bellwork:

1. Monitor student work by walking around the room
2. Use a timer, especially at the beginning of the year.
3. Check the work. Have students use a different colored pen or pencil to mark if their response is correct with a √ or to write the correct answer if incorrect.
4. Develop a bellwork quiz given at regular intervals where students use only their bellwork to answer the questions.
5. Use questions from the bellwork on a test.
6. For questions with no one correct answer, ask several students to read their answers.
7. Collect bellwork weekly or grade notebooks and include bellwork as a criterion.

Activity

3.1 Examine your textbook and curriculum guide. Develop bellwork for one week that corresponds to your content.

II.   Spaced Reviews and Distributed Practice

It's very frustrating to work really hard at teaching a concept only to find out two weeks after the unit was completed that your students don't remember any of it! You can, however, minimize this frustration by using two techniques. End of lesson reviews and weekly reviews are effective ways to increase retention and student learning. You should insert reviews at various points in your lessons as well as throughout the week. You might start the lesson with a review of previous learnings, summarize within the lesson and finish the lesson with a review. You don't have to do all three in every lesson, but its important to consciously plan to review.

There are a variety of techniques that can be used for reviews:
- Students write in their notebooks a summary of the learning
- Pair students and each gives two important points of the lesson
- Have small groups discuss review questions
- Play a game, i.e. jeopardy
- Bellwork is also an effective beginning of lesson review technique.

Long-term retention is enhanced by distributed practice, that is, providing students with opportunities to practice previously learned skills or information over time. So, if students are practicing fractions, include problems on a previously learned skill, such as percent or division in their bellwork or homework. Here are a few other suggestions:

1.   Develop crossword puzzles that include "old" vocabulary/spelling words.
2.   Incorporate 1-2 questions on previous content in homework and/or handouts
3.   Use games such as bingo, jeopardy, relays, etc. to review new and previous content

III.   Active Learning

Most people think active learning means students are up and doing something like role playing, a science experiment, or working on a project. While all these are, indeed, examples of active learning, we can expand the definition of active learning to include the *engagement of the minds of the learners*. With this broader definition, we can include mental activities as "active" learning.

Active participation can take three forms: overt, covert, and a combination of both. Let's look at examples of these forms.

> I hear and I forget. I see and I remember. I do and I understand.-Chinese Proverb

Overt active learning is observable. Directions from the teacher include: draw, write, show, tell. Covert learning is non-observable and includes such directions as think, imagine, pretend, visualize, listen. The combination of overt and covert might sound like: "Think about ... and write...;" "Remember a time...discuss with your group...;" "Pretend you're the character_____ and act out how you would have responded."

Bomwell and Eison (1991) describe active learning as having certain characteristics:

- Students are involved in more than listening
- Less emphasis is placed on transmitting information and more on developing students' skills
- Students are involved in higher-order thinking
- Students are engaged in activities, i.e. reading, discussing, writing
- Greater emphasis is placed on students' exploration of their own attitudes and values

They define active learning as *anything that involves students in doing things and thinking about the things they are doing.* This is not to say that students cannot learn from reading text or from listening to a lecture. But if our goal is more than the transmission of information and we want to connect the student to the content, then we must consider more active methods of instruction.

Edgar Dale(1969) said the percent of information we remember is tied to our level of involvement with the information. Look at his Cone of Learning below:

Retention Rate	Activity	
10 % retention	Reading	
20 % retention	Hearing Words	
30% retention	Looking at Pictures	
50% retention	Watching a Movie Looking at an Exhibit Watching a Demonstration Seeing it Done on Location	Passive
70% retention	Participating in a Discussion Giving a Talk	Active
90 % retention	Doing a Dramatic Presentation Simulating the Real Experience Doing the Real Thing	

According to this model, students who merely read information will retain only 10 % of that information. If we lecture on that material, they will retain 20%. And if the students discuss the information in cooperative groups or pairs, they will retain 70% of the information. Knowing this, can we justify assigning reading material without discussion and hope our students will understand it? And can we support giving a lecture, no matter how "great" we are, and assume students will understand and retain the information without any follow-up discussion or additional learning experiences? Active learning is an essential component to your lessons if you want to increase student comprehension and retention.

Activity

3.2 Think about lessons in which you were engaged and interested. Describe one of those lessons. What active learning characteristics did the teacher employ?

Activity

3.3 Examine the lesson plan below and identify the ways the teacher has incorporated active learning.

Subject: Nutrition and Health
Objective: The student will a.) describe the Food Guide Pyramid; and b.) use the pyramid to plan a healthy diet.

Procedure:
1. Bellwork (on transparency): *Think about a nutrition label. Now answer these questions: "What kind of information is on a nutrition label? If you haven't seen one, what kind of information should be on it?" Be prepared to share with the class.*
2. After sharing their bellwork answers, students silently read the text section on the food pyramid and answer questions on the reading guide.
3. In small groups, students write a list of favorite foods and then classify the foods according to the pyramid.
4. Small groups develop 3 healthy meals and 2 snacks for one day.
5. Homework: Keep track of what you eat for one day. Classify the foods according to the food pyramid.

While one lesson might not have <u>all</u> these activities, you can see how the inclusion of active learning strategies makes for a more interesting lesson.

IV.   Nonlinguistic Representations

Nonlinguistic representations are imagery forms. There are five ways to generate nonlinguistic representations: using graphic organizers, making physical models, creating mental visual pictures, drawing pictures, and employing kinesthetic activities.

Graphic organizers combine linguistic and nonlinguistic forms of learning. They usually have symbols and arrows or lines to show relationships. Six common organizers are descriptive, cause and effect, comparison-contrast, main idea and details, sequence of events, and a concept pattern.

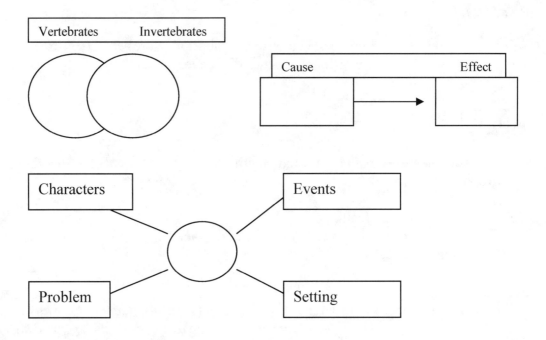

Physical models are concrete representations of the information students are learning. Making a model of the cell using play dough, creating a diorama of a story, or using Styrofoam balls to design a replica of an atom are examples of physical models.

Mental pictures also help students learn abstract concepts. Asking students to visualize or to imagine leads students to develop these mental pictures. Carefully script the visualization, reading slowly so the students actually "see" the concept. To encourage visualizations, tell students to relax and close their eyes. Visualizing a scene in a story, being a water molecule in the water cycle, imagining a soldier in a battle, or seeing a pizza cut into eighths, are all ways to "be" there. After guiding the imagery, ask students to talk about their images and what questions came to mind.

Whenever possible, students should draw or color pictures which represent a concept. Students might develop pictures for the steps of the scientific process, draw a map of the world or illustrate a scene from a story. Drawing can be group or individual projects, completed in a journal, on the board, or on poster paper.

Finally, students can engage in physical activities to help understand a concept. Students might physically demonstrate different fractions, population density, or the planets of our solar system. This technique requires space, which classrooms might not have, and may limit your use of this strategy.

Using a variety of these techniques can help students learn and remember information in a more active manner.

V.   Learning Styles

Everyone prefers to learn in a certain modality- visual, auditory, kinesthetic or tactile. A visual learner prefers to take in information by seeing, watching, and reading. For the auditory learner information is best processed through speaking and listening. A kinesthetic learner prefers physical activity involving the large muscle groups and the tactile learner likes small body movement, body sensations and emotional involvement.

For example, visual learners like seeing videotapes and demonstrations, drawing, reading, and making graphic organizers. The auditory learners prefer lectures, oral presentations, reading aloud, and discussions. The kinesthetic students like using manipulatives, doing hands-on activities, writing on the board, and using hand signals to answer questions. The tactile student enjoys working with concrete objectives, cooperative learning groups, taking notes, and small group discussions.

In general, these four learning styles appear in our general population in the following percentages: visual – 35-40%, auditory – 10-15%, kinesthetic – 25-35% and tactile – 15-25% (Performance Learning Systems, 2007). What does this mean for teachers? We tend to teach in the manner that we prefer to learn because this is our comfort zone. If we are strong visual learners, we will teach to that preferential learning modality. Unfortunately, if we do this, then we're ignoring the learning needs of 60% of the learners in our classroom. Research suggests that effective teachers try to incorporate a broad variety of learning styles beyond their own (Doolan & Honigsfeld, 2000)

Your classes will have a wide diversity of learners and, chances are, even after your most creative and well-structured lesson, someone won't "get it". Knowing students' learning preferences is not as important as recognizing that all learning styles will be present in your classroom. So, what do you do?

As you plan a lesson, consider the four modalities. For example, you could present the information using the text or some reading material or video, write on the board using colored markers for emphasis while students take notes, have students discuss the material in cooperative groups and incorporate a lab or other type of hands-on activity. You can reteach a lesson in the same way you initially presented it or you can adapt your teaching to increase the probability that more students will learn. Using this approach, students who do not "get it" one way are apt to understand the information in a different modality. You can also see the value of repeated exposure to the information. It is up to you to adapt your basic lesson plan to meet the needs of your students.

Activity

3.4 Examine your curriculum or scope and sequence for the first few weeks of school and design a lesson that incorporates at least one active learning strategy discussed thus far.

VI.   Questioning

No matter what you teach or what grade level you teach or the level of your students, effective questioning is a necessary component of your lessons. Questions can serve several purposes: they reinforce learning, promote higher level thinking, help you diagnose student learning problems and help you evaluate your own teaching. (Silverman & Shearer, 1985).

Effective teachers use questions to:
- relate the new lesson to previous learning
- clarify points within the lesson
- check students' comprehension
- develop higher order thinking skills
- summarize or review

Good questions have certain characteristics.

Characteristic	Effective Example	Ineffective Example
Concise and to the point with one strong idea. There should be just one question posed at a time.	What happened to Jack?	What happened to Jack, why was this important, and how did his actions affect others in the story? Anyone?
Short enough for students to understand and remember.	Think about technology. What are some good things and some bad things about technology?	What are the pros and cons of technology? In other words, is there some good along with the bad? Some people think computers are a good thing but others believe it isolates people and we're losing our sense of community.
Clearly stated in language students understand.	How did people view the US government during the Vietnam War and the Gulf War?	Compare the Vietnam War and the Gulf War on their impact to societal views on the US governmental policies and global economy.
Require more than a simple "yes" or "no" answer.	What did you learn about global warming?	Do you think global warming is real?
Stated in a way that the answer is not suggested.	What is the sequence of steps in the water cycle?	The water cycle is continuous. Water evaporates and returns to earth. Some scientists suggest that the water we have on our planet today is the same water that was here 4 billion years ago. What happens in the water cycle?

We can classify questions as high- or low-order. Both types of questions can be used with all ages and achievement levels. Using Bloom's cognitive taxonomy, we can classify the knowledge level questions as low-order. These questions, which are considered a fundamental level of comprehension, focus on recall or memory. Most of these questions deal with facts, such as, who, what, when, how and where. Questions at this fundamental level require the learner to repeat, recall or recognize previously learned material. Tasks such as matching, listing, naming, identifying, labeling, and choosing are all low-order thinking skills.

Whenever the learner is asked to use the information in some way, then we are requiring a higher order of thinking. At Bloom's comprehension level, the student explains, rephrases, infers, gives an example, or concludes. The student must do more than repeat what he/she already read or heard. The application level requires the student to solve problems using his knowledge. When we ask students to compare or contrast, to analyze a story or character or to examine the issues, we are using Bloom's analysis level. The synthesis or creative level involves developing a new plan, writing an new ending or an original story, or designing an experiment. Evaluation, as the name implies, asks the learner to judge the worth or value of something with a given standard. Here's a chart illustrating questions corresponding to Bloom's cognitive levels:

Bloom's Cognitive Level	Sample Questions
Knowledge	What is…? Where is…? When did…? Who…? List…? Define… Can you recall…? How would you describe…?
Comprehension (Understanding)	What is the main idea of…? Explain… Summarize… How would you classify…? Give an example of…
Application	How would you solve ___ using what you've learned…? What would happen if…? What plan would you use…?
Analysis	How are ___ and ___ alike/different…? What inference…? What conclusion can you draw…? What was the motive…?
Synthesis (Creative)	Create a new… How would you design…? What might happen if…? How could you test for…? Create a new ending…
Evaluation	What would be better…? How could you determine…? What judgment can you make…? How would you select…?

Most teachers' manuals today provide numerous questions from which to select. If your text does not have a sufficient number of higher-order questions, you should create your own to enhance your students' thinking. You should plan your questions thoughtfully and write them into your lesson plan. Leaving questioning to chance may not produce the results you desire.

In the typical question-answer interchange, the teacher asks a question, a student answers, and the teacher praises or corrects. You can modify the Q&A technique in a few simple ways (Kagan, 1999):

Think-Pair-Share

In Think-Pair-Share, the teacher poses a question, directs students to "think" about their answer, and then pair with another student to share their ideas. After a short time, the teacher randomly asks pairs to share with the whole class.

Partners Compare

After a 10-15 minute learning segment, the teacher asks a question. Student pairs are formed. One student contributes his/her ideas to their partner, and the partner paraphrases or restates the idea before contributing his own ideas. They reverse roles with subsequent questions. .

Heads Together

In Heads Together, students are in small groups. The teacher poses the question, provides think time, and the group members put their heads "together" to arrive at an answer. The teacher calls on the groups for their answers.

For a variation on this technique, the groups might write their answer on a small white eraser board or slate. Instead of calling on individual groups for an oral response, the groups hold up their board on the teacher's signal.

Think-Write-Pair-Share

A Think-Write-Share is a variation of Think-Pair-Share where students write down their thoughts following the teacher's query and then pair and share with another student.

Team Quiz (Thiagarajan, 2005)

Following a lecture, reading, film or other learning experience, divide the class into teams of 3-4 students. Ask the teams to review notes, etc. and develop 3 questions for which there is a definite correct answer. Give students 3-5 minutes to develop their questions. At the end of the time period, select one team at random and ask its spokesperson to read one of their questions. The questioning team selects an individual from any other team to answer. If correct, his/her team gets 2 points (or any value you select). If incorrect, the team loses one point. Then select another team to ask a question.

Say Something (Short, et. al., 1996)

Either at predetermined intervals or at the end of the learning experience, provide students an opportunity to say something about the content. Provide students with a prompt and have them work in pairs.

Possible prompts:	Why did…	I don't get…
	What does this mean?	I think that…
	I wonder if…	This is important because…

3.5 Change the low-level question on the left to a higher-level question. The first one is done for you.

Low-Level Question	Higher-Lever Question
Who was George Washington?	Why is George Washington called the *Father of our Country*?
What 3 pieces of information can you find on a food label?	
Name four American Presidents in the 20th century.	
What is global warming?	
Who wrote *Romeo and Juliet*?	

Wait Time

Wait time is the length of time the teacher waits for a student to answer a question before responding or going on to another student. Research indicates that teachers who wait from 3 to 5 seconds after asking a question, usually get better responses from their students and better learning results. Wait time allows students to think about the question, understand what is being asked, and formulate a response.

Teachers either jump in too soon after posing a question to provide the answer or they give hints, such as, "Remember yesterday's lesson?" So, the preferred technique for a question-answer activity is to ask one single question, wait (silence), call on a student, wait (silence), and respond. Here's an example:

Teacher – Who is the main character in this story? (wait) Tammy?
Tammy – Palmer
Teacher – (wait) Yes. Are there any other important characters? (wait) Nick?

A 3- second wait time after a question can seem like an eternity, especially if no one's hand rises in response. When students call out answers, it may appear that that the class is engaged and we might find that preferable to silence. However, it seems logical that if students are calling out answers then there is no wait time and, thus, no think time.

If, after asking a question, the student responds with, *I don't know*, find out if they don't understand the question or truly don't know. Here's how that would sound:

Teacher – How does an earthquake occur? (wait) Jacob?
Jacob – I don't know.
Teacher – (wait) Is the question unclear?
Jacob – No, I just don't know.

Teacher – OK, well, Jacob, what happens on the earth's surface during an earthquake? (wait)

Jacob – shaking

Teacher – (wait) Yes, that's correct. So what causes that shaking? (wait) Brooke?

Call-outs are common, especially when students are excited about a lesson or really want your attention. To minimize call outs, here are some things to say:

Raise your hand so I can call on you.
Think first, then raise your hand if you have an answer to this question.
I'm going to ask some questions and if you know the answer, raise your hand.

If students call out, it's best not recognize them. If, after you call on another student who gives their response, they say, *That's what I said!* reply with, *But you didn't have your hand raised.*

Call outs are inevitable, but if you value wait time, try to minimize them as much as possible. A handy way to ensure that you use wait time is to mentally count to 3. You can also write the word "WAIT" on a 3x5 card or sticky note and place it where you can see it during your lesson. Your silence after asking a question is invaluable to student learning.

Responding to students' answers

Asking a well-developed question and using wait time is just the first part of Q&A. It is really important that you listen to what your students say in response to your questions. It's just not enough to nod, smile or say, "Good." You need to listen carefully to the answers without interrupting them unless they are straying far off course, are totally unfocused, or are being disruptive.

There are two possibilities in a Q & A interchange: the student may give the correct answer or an incorrect one. With correct answers, you will need to acknowledge that their answer is correct and provide positive reinforcement. Generally, you should only repeat a student's answer when the other students may not have heard the answer, and you should phrase it as *Pete said...* If the student's answer is incorrect, then they should be told it's incorrect and given feedback. All students should know why an answer is correct or incorrect.

Levels of Feedback (Crane, S.)

1. Confirmation	Informs the learner of the accuracy of the response. Used to reinforce correct answers; does not tell why a response is correct or incorrect.	*That's right.* *No. That's not correct.* *Yes.* *Good*
2. Correction	Informs the learner the response was incorrect and gives the correct response.	*No, the answer is _____.*
3. Explanation	Feedback here includes a rationale for the correct response. It is designed to correct misconceptions.	*No, the answer is ____ because...* *No, let's look at the procedure again...*
4. Diagnosis	This type of feedback examines the error.	*No, you forgot to regroup.* *Your answer is not right because you forgot ...*
5. Elaboration	This feedback provides additional information. It is designed to extend the learner's knowledge base. This is provided with both correct and incorrect responses.	*Yes, that's correct. And did you also know that...*

What if the student's answer is really off base? You might try to find something positive to stress about the answer:

      a. identify the aspect of the answer that is correct (*The first part is correct...*);

      b. suggest a question that would fit the answer (*Close. If I had asked for the protagonist, you would be right.*);

      c. focus on the thinking process (*You're thinking along the right track.*)

Other techniques you can use with incorrect answers are:

Probes – *Tell me more*   This probe requires the student to elaborate on the response given to an earlier question. Such probes indicate to the learner that their answer was in the right direction but was not adequate.

     What do you mean when you say...? This is useful when the student's response is unclear or incomplete.

     Can you give me an example? Or *Where is that in the reading?* If you need some insight into the student's thinking, use this probe, as it can reveal an error in thinking.

Slice - This is a technique to reduce the scope of the question. If you asked for three examples, slice the question with: *Can you give me one example of ...*

Perhaps you asked for the steps in the writing process and were met with blank stares. You can slice the question with the following: *Let's start with the first step. Do you remember the first step?*

If you asked a question and there is complete silence and no one responds or if several students respond to the question incorrectly, then:

4. Rephrase the question (maybe they didn't understand it)
5. Review the pertinent information needed to answer the question (they may need a refresher)
6. Model your thinking (always effective in teaching students how to think)

When a student says something silly or off the wall, you must refrain from using sarcasm, reprimands, accusations, and personal attacks. These tactics can destroy the type of classroom climate you want in order to have a successful question-answer interchange. Just get them back on track with, *Let's focus on the question.*

Activity

3.6 Pretend that your class read *Goldilocks and the Three Bears* and you are checking their comprehension. How would you respond to the following student answers?

1. Teacher – What is the setting of the story?
   Student 1 – A house

Your response _____

2. Teacher – What happened in the story?
   (Silence)

Your response _____

3. Teacher – What type of person is Goldilocks?
   Student 2 – Mean
   Student 3 – Pretty

Your response _____

4. Teacher – Is this a good story?
   All mumble either "yes" or "no"

Your response _____

3.7 Create a lesson plan that incorporates effective questioning described in this chapter. Write and sequence your core questions and possible probes. Don't forget to focus on the learning objective as you plan! Use the form that follows.

Lesson Plan

Subject: _____ Date _____

Objective: The student will _____

_____

What knowledge/skills do students need prior to this lesson?

How will student mastery be determined?

Teacher Actions	Student Actions
Introducing the Lesson	
Presenting the Lesson	
Closing the Lesson	

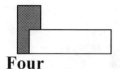

The mind is not a vessel
to be filled, but a fire
to be ignited.-Plutarch

Four

Monitoring Learning and Adjusting Instruction

You taught a great lesson and now you're wondering, *Did my students reach the learning objective? How do I know if they met the objective and if they didn't, what do I do now?* It's a terrible sensation when you spent hours working on a particular unit, creating motivating lessons, and find, to your dismay, that your students did not demonstrate a high level of understanding based on your unit test. You must remember that there are many reasons why students do not perform well on tests—one being the test itself.

However, to avoid poor performance on a summative test because they didn't understand the content, teachers need to constantly monitor students' learning. When student learning falls short of the desired goal you will need to adjust your instruction.

Monitoring and adjusting is important in almost all fields. Take your doctor, for example. Your doctor will prescribe a treatment, and then monitor your vitals and blood work to see if the treatment is working. If the results are not as desired, your doctor will prescribe a new treatment. That's monitoring and adjusting. A business must analyze its income and expenses to ensure that the expenses do not exceed the income. If the results of such study are not satisfactory, then modifications must be made to the budget. That's monitoring and adjusting.

Monitoring includes all the activities practiced by teachers to keep an eye on student learning in order to make instructional decisions and to give feedback to students on their progress. In education we often call "monitoring" formative evaluation. Its purpose is to tell you how well students are progressing toward the objective(s). Monitoring requires that you gather evidence from <u>all</u> learners while the lesson is taking place. Effective monitoring tells us who is struggling, the curricular areas we need to emphasize, and the instructional methods that are not working. We cannot wait until the end of the unit to find out through a summative test if one or more of our students didn't reach the learning objective.

How do you accomplish this monitoring? Just as your doctor monitors your vital signs, you must observe your students. You need to elicit some form of observable behavior from your students during the lesson or at various points during the unit. Examples of monitoring include (Cotton, 1988):

- Questioning
- Circulating during seatwork and observing student work
- Engaging in one-on-one conversations with students
- Assigning, collecting and correcting homework
- Reviewing periodically

The purpose of monitoring is formative in nature. That means you will use the information to correct the learning environment in order to increase learning. Some techniques might be as simple as asking a question and calling for a show of hands. This feedback is immediate and allows you to tailor your lesson and activities to the needs of your students. Other kinds of feedback may be written and collected. In these cases, you must review the material prior to the next class session and use the results to guide future classes.

There are a number of monitoring techniques that you can use. These methods can be used to measure students' mastery of complex skills, knowledge of facts, grasp of concepts, and/or application of principles. No matter what form your monitoring takes, it should inform you about your students' progress toward mastery of the instructional objectives.

Methods of Monitoring Progress

Let's look at some methods of monitoring student learning.

- ## Questioning

Probably the easiest and most used method for finding out the level of students' understanding is questioning. You must keep in mind, however, that asking: *Are there any questions?* is not monitoring. Also the traditional Q and A where one student at a time answers your questions only provides you feedback for the students who answered your questions. The way to check if and how many of your students understand is to use some form of **every pupil response**, or visible quiz. Here are a few techniques:

Thumbs Up – Students respond to a whole class question by putting their thumbs up if they understand, thumbs down if they do not understand or thumbs to the side if they are confused. You can also use this technique after a student has answered a question and you ask if the class "agrees" with the answer.

> To get new knowledge requires new questions. – John Evanson

Signal Cards – Students use a card to indicate the answer.
Cards may be True/False or lettered A, B, C, D for multiple choice questions.

Fist of Five – Students show the number of fingers that corresponds to their level of understanding (one being the lowest, five the highest). This method can also be used to show level of agreement with a student's answer or the answer in a multiple choice question.

Response Boards – Students use white boards or write-on boards to display their answer to a question. Can't afford white boards? Use scrap paper or insert white paper into a page protector. (If you use white boards or the page protector method you'll have to buy dry erase markers.) Response boards are very useful with either individual or group responses.

One-Minute Paper – On a half-sheet of paper or a 3x5 card, students write their responses to a question or prompt. Student names aren't necessary and these aren't graded because your purpose is to determine if the class understands what was taught. To use this feedback method, use very specific questions. Display one question, have students write for one minute, and collect their responses as they leave the room. Prompts might include:

> List two key ideas from today's lesson.
> What three things did you learn today?
> What was the most important thing in today's lesson?
> Write the procedure for solving…
> Write two quiz questions and the answers on today's class.
> What question(s) do you have about today's class?

Your task then is to tabulate their responses, make note of useful comments, and talk about the results in the next class meeting.

- ## Circulating During Seatwork and Observing Student Work

Effective teachers monitor students during seatwork. This means, they move around the classroom observing how well or poorly their students are progressing with their assignment. Effective teachers do not wait for students to ask for help, but, rather, initiate interactions with their students to encourage, correct, and reinforce. They work with students on a one-to-one basis as needed.

The general purpose of independent seatwork and homework is for students to practice newly presented material. It is generally accepted that for seatwork to be most effective, teachers should tell students the purpose and relevance of the practice activity. In addition, the directions for seatwork must be clear so that students work at least at an 80% success rate. To ensure this high level of success, you should work the first one or two questions/problems together with the class.

> A child miseducated is a child lost.-John F. Kennedy

When you find a student struggling or not completing the work correctly, try to avoid just saying, *"No, that's not right."* It's more inviting language to say, *"Let's look at this one again,"* or *"Let's think about what we talked about earlier."* Then guide the student using questions such as "How" and "Why." In your monitoring of the class, if you notice that many students are having the same problem, stop the seatwork and reteach the material. Begin with, *"I noticed several of you have the same questions. Let's review…"*

Monitoring seatwork doesn't just apply to paper-pencil independent work. Effective teachers circulate the room during labs, cooperative group work, and pair work. Some teachers call it "Monitoring while roaming around." It's safe to say that effective teaching doesn't occur when you are sitting behind your desk.

It's also a good idea to provide cues while the students work. For example, you might say: *"You should be on page 2 by now,"* or *"You have 10 minutes left,"* or *"You should have finished the chart. If not, move on to the next part."* Seatwork should be collected and scored. Some teachers use peer-scoring methods, but papers are still turned in for the teacher to review and record a grade. You might not record a letter grade in your gradebook, per se, but you should indicate "completion" of the assignment with a check (√). Some teachers assign unfinished seatwork as homework. If you do this, be sure students turn in this work upon entering the next class because if you forget, they will "forget" to finish it the next time it's assigned.

Activity

4.1 Design a seatwork activity for the first week of school. Try to anticipate problems your students might have with the activity and consider ways to deal with those problems.

- **Engaging in one-on-one conversations with students**

Short, brief conferences with students are often the most efficient way to determine why they are not progressing and/or learning. Conferencing is best done during class time while your other students are engaged in independent seatwork. Conferences, like lessons, should be planned. You need to think about the following:

- What do you hope to accomplish?
- What data/information are you going to share with the student?
- How will you begin the conference?

It's best to focus on one or two issues for a conference. Let's say Amber never turns in homework, makes marginal scores on tests, seldom comes prepared for class, and often daydreams during seatwork. You can't change all these behaviors so you need to pick the one with which you might have success.

Call the student to your desk, invite them to sit down and begin by saying, *"I noticed you haven't turned in the last three homework assignments."* Now wait! Let the student talk. After all, this is a student-teacher conference. Listen to what the student says. Try to avoid lecturing and, instead, summarize what the student is saying, *"So you didn't understand..."*

> If a child can't learn the way we teach, maybe we should teach the way they learn. – Ignacio Estrada

or *"You don't have time to study at home."* Then try to develop a plan and say something like, *"Aside from canceling all future assignments, how can I help you the next time?"* At this point, you might give specific study advice, reteach a problem area indicated by the student, or decide on a strategy *("OK, I'll move your seat closer to the front of the room.")*. Thank the student for being honest and emphasize that you want to help him/her be successful. Don't forget to follow up your conference by providing positive reinforcement when your student meets the goal you set.

These conferences should not last longer than 5 minutes and students should not feel they are at the Inquisition. This is a time for you to establish a positive relationship with your students, demonstrate that you care about their progress, and get information that may help you teach more effectively.

- ## Assigning, collecting and correcting homework

Homework is another method of providing students with practice opportunities and should not be an afterthought in your planning. The research on homework indicates that it should be a focused strategy with the goal of increasing student understanding. As a monitoring device, homework can provide you with information on students who did not understand the concept or skills introduced in class. In addition to being focused on a goal, homework, to be successful, should be collected and commented on by the teacher.

There are generally four types of homework (Rutherford, 2002):
   a) Practice – helps students master skills and reinforce in-class learning. Leads to memorization of basic rules, algorithms, or laws so the skill becomes automatic.
   b) Creative – promotes critical thinking and problem solving skills.
   c) Extension – helps students deepen their understanding of a concept.
   d) Preparation – helps students prepare for the next day's lesson or an upcoming unit. Prior knowledge should be high for this type of homework.
It is important to align the type of homework assignment to the learning goal. As with seatwork, students should be made aware of the purpose of the homework assignment.

According to Marzano (2001) we can draw four key generalizations from the research on homework.

1. The amount of homework should vary according to the grade level of the student. Generally, homework at the elementary levels has not produced strong effects on achievement but it has at the high school level. That does not mean that elementary students in grades 2-5 should not be given homework. It is believed by proponents that small amounts can strengthen young students' study skills. So, then, how much homework is appropriate? Experts suggest the *10-minute rule*: about 10 minutes a night beginning in grade one with an additional 10 minutes each year. Therefore, a student in grade 7 can handle 70 minutes total of homework a night. Yes, total! This is not 70 minutes per subject! The chart below provides another guideline for homework (Cooper, H., 1989).

Grade Level	Amount of homework
1-3	One to three assignments per week taking 15 minutes or less
4-6	Two to four 15-45 minute assignments a week
7-9	Three to five 45-75 minute assignments a week
10-12	Four to five 75-120 minutes assignments a week

Why consider the amount of homework? Too much homework might produce negative effects such as a loss of interest and copying from other students. What is far more important than time, however, is the quality of the homework assignment. The assignment should match the students' independent level of learning and, as with seatwork, directions should be reviewed and one or two examples should be worked with the students so they know how to proceed on their own.

2. <u>Parent involvement</u> should be kept to a minimum. Parents should "facilitate" homework but not try to "do" the homework with their child. If a student needs help with the homework content, that could be a signal that the assignment is too difficult or was not understood. You can't control parental involvement, but you can make sure the assignment is one the child can complete on his/her own.

3. The <u>purpose</u> of the homework assignment should be made clear to the student. If homework is for the purpose of practice, then it should be structured around content with which students are highly familiar. This seems logical. Yet, teachers will assign homework on material that has not been introduced thinking the students can figure it out on their own. Try to avoid the latter as much as possible.

It's also important to make sure the students have the materials at home to complete the assignment. Before you assign work that involves research on the Internet, be sure all students have access to a computer. If you want students to draw and color a diagram, make sure they all have the coloring materials needed. If you know some students do not have the necessary materials, assemble a homework baggie with the resources they will need and let students check them out from the classroom.

4. Teachers should <u>collect and comment</u> on homework. While putting a grade alone increases the effectiveness of homework on learning, both a grade and a comment together have the highest effect on learning. Timely feedback improves student learning so it's best to give constructive comments within one or two days after a homework assignment is completed. Not all homework should receive the same level of feedback by the teacher. Some experts recommend that homework be checked for completion and grades should be given intermittently. Some teachers prefer to review completed assignments using peer scoring and then collecting and recording

> If you can't make a mistake, you can't make anything.- Marva Collins

grades. What is important to note is that you should collect and record a grade (accuracy or completeness), and provide feedback comments to improve student performance.

In reviewing and grading the homework, you should notice common errors or faulty thinking on the part of your students. As you return the homework, communicate with your students what you observed in their work. If there were common errors among your students, use it as the basis of your bellwork for the next class.

If a number of students do not complete their assignments, you should hold a one-on-one conference with them to find out why. Be sure to emphasize that you cannot help them unless you can see the areas in which they're having difficulty, and that's one purpose of homework.

Activity

4.2 Develop a homework policy to share with your students and their parents. Be sure to include how often homework might be assigned, how absences will be handled, and how homework will be used in the student's final grade.

- ## Reviewing Periodically

Probably the simplest way to integrate regular reviews is through the use of bellwork, or "do nows," conducted at the beginning of class. Questions on new material from the previous day's lesson can help to determine if reteaching is needed. There are several commercially prepared review programs designated by content area and grade level. In addition, today's teacher's manuals, include review questions that you can adapt as bellwork or include on handouts.

Another way to review is with games. Teachers have adapted games such as Jeopardy, baseball, tic-tac-toe, Concentration, and Bingo, etc. as review methods. If you're going to use games as a monitoring device, be sure you're listening to students' responses to the questions. You'll want to note what questions are missed, which students seem to be having the greatest difficulty, and what concept areas give your students the most trouble.

Activity

4.3 Search online, or think about your favorite games, and design a review in your subject area to be implemented in the first month of school. This review might consist of last year's content to be used in the first week of school.

Adjusting Instruction

Effective teachers are constantly evaluating their students' learning, and, in fact, learning and assessment are often indistinguishable. The previous section on monitoring stressed the need to evaluate learning as instruction was ongoing, because, as we know, it is dangerous to assess at the end of a unit of instruction, only to discover that your students didn't "get it."

> There are really no mistakes in life -- only lessons. Anonymous

The best guarantee that your students will understand and achieve the learning objectives is good instruction. But, let's say your students did not understand the concept or skill. Generally, after you've determined what your students did not learn, you can reteach, back up and review, teach prerequisite knowledge/skills, or go on. If only a few students did not "get it," you could provide a peer tutor, work with the small group, provide tutoring before or after school, or provide some other form of support (teacher assistant, computer assisted instruction). It's easy to say, "*Ok. I'll just go over it again.*" But using the same methods with the same content may not produce the learning you want. When you reflect on your instruction and how you need to adjust it, you should examine three areas: content, teaching method, and product.

Content

Content refers to what we teach and what we want our students to understand or be able to do. The essential elements in content are objectives, student readiness, and materials used to reach those objectives. Your first step might be to reexamine the objectives and determine if the instructional concepts to be mastered are broad based. Learning should be focused on the essential key concepts and principals rather than a long string of minute skills. If you believe the content is "too much," or there are too many objectives, you should focus your instruction on the key concepts. For example, rather than have students memorize a list of American Civil War generals, emphasize the causes and results of the war.

There are many ways to access the same information and if you think the materials are outside the students' instructional reading levels, then you need to find a variety of text and resource materials. While you were provided with a standard curriculum text, there may be library books and public print media (magazines, newspapers) that can be used to teach the same concepts. Educational videos and DVDs as well as manipulative materials, lab materials, and learning games can also be utilized. The Internet offers a plethora of information on different topics and concepts that can be used to supplement your text.

> Our children need to be treated as human beings- exquisite, complex and elegant in their diversity.-Lloyd Dennis

Your students may not possess the background knowledge or interest to be successful. If this is the case, you must consider developing that background. Background information includes necessary vocabulary and foundation concepts or skills that will help students understand the new information. If your students are going to read historical fiction, then you might need to provide the historical backdrop. When possible, use the Internet for student research to develop background knowledge and interest levels. There are technological techniques you can integrate into your curriculum, including WebQuest (http://webquest.org) and TrackStar (http://trackstar.4teachers.org) that will help prepare your students for the new learning.

Method

If the desired level of learning did not occur because of the teaching **method**, you will need to reteach using a different process. When you reteach, you should avoid presenting the information in the same way as you did initially. (If it didn't work the first time, why use the same technique?) Create new questions and provide different examples and nonexamples in your new lesson. If you didn't use group methods, try paired or cooperative learning groups.

Try to incorporate the use of graphic organizers, diagrams or charts to increase their understanding. One method of differentiating assignments, valuable in reteaching, is to use tiered instruction (Tomlinson, 2000). This is a method of teaching one concept while meeting the different learning needs in a group. In this approach, you would develop at least three activities to teach the same concept to meet the needs of average, above average and below average learners in your classroom.

Sometimes the students just didn't get enough time with the material or did not have enough practice. Learning centers and/or computer stations can provide students additional practice toward the desired learning objective. If possible, find old textbooks that provide the same information in a different format to give additional practice activities. Placed in files for student use, these can be included in centers or practice folders.

A very simple approach to enhancing comprehension is to introduce questions *during* the presentation rather than waiting until the end. This would include stopping at predetermined points to ask questions during a reading, lecture, demonstration, and even during a video. If you're reteaching, break-up the presentation into smaller units (than in the original) and use more, and different, questions throughout.

Many teachers use Think Alouds (Tierney, Readence, & Dishner, 2004; Santa, Havens, & Valdes, 2004) as a modeling strategy in both initial and reteaching strategies. In modeling skills or thinking processes, the teacher takes on the role of learner and describes for the students how he/she initiates or solves a task. For example, a reading teacher might describe what she does when she encounters an unknown work; a math teacher might demonstrate how she analyzes a word problem; and a science teacher might show how he connects a concept to current events.

Product

Product is the output. It is the measure of student learning. It's seatwork, homework, spelling tests, essays, and projects. Sometimes students do not perform well on the product, or output, because it was too complex or too ambiguous. For some students, asking them to "*Draw a book jacket*" for a book report is too unclear, or when we ask them to create a model of the universe, they don't know where to start. While you might think that giving general, vague instructions might allow for more creativity, unfortunately, some students need the specifics and without them, they get stuck.

With complex projects that will take two weeks or longer, consider writing down the steps students will have to take for successful completion and include a time line. For projects, such as that book jacket that you'd thought would be fun, consider giving students a list of what to include (author, title, picture of an event from the book, a synopsis, etc.)

You need to consider your time requirements given the amount of work. Asking students to complete 50 math problems may be excessive, especially if the time limit is not sufficient. Let's suppose that you have a handout with a number of questions or vocabulary terms for the students to answer. Rather than have each student do the entire handout, a jigsaw group (Kagan, 1994) might make the task more manageable. Each student in the group is assigned a certain number of questions, etc. and is responsible for sharing the information with the other members of the group. A high school history teacher divided her handout review questions in half and each row of students was assigned one of the halves. After 20 minutes, the students buddied-up to share their findings. The Jigsaw method is extremely flexible and can be used successfully with large group projects, too.

A learning agenda (Kluth, 2005) is another way to modify the product. An agenda is a list of activities or projects the student must complete in a specific period of time. Some activities may be required of all students with other activities chosen from a list. A middle school language arts teacher used a learning agenda for spelling practice. In the spelling agenda, all students were required to locate the definitions and write a meaningful sentence for the week's spelling list. Students then chose from a list of varied activities that included: make a word search, create a crossword puzzle, or write a short story using the word list. By providing an agenda, you are giving students multiple means to the content, accommodating different achievement levels and allowing for student choice. Learning agendas can be used with the whole class or individual students and are particularly effective with special needs students.

> The pupil who is never required to do what he cannot do, never does what he can do. – John Stuart Mill

Introducing a reteaching lesson

The manner in which you present a reteaching lesson is just as important as the activity you planned. Consider the following scenario: Mr. Valdez stands at the front of the room and says, *"You bombed on the homework. Scores were abysmal! So today, we're going to go over it again."* If you were a student in this classroom, how would you feel? You probably wouldn't be too receptive to the lesson since you've just been chastised. It's important to be honest without being sarcastic or demeaning. What if Mr. Valdez had said: *"The scores didn't represent what you have learned. Seventy percent of the class missed questions 5 and 6. After we review the entire assignment, let's spend some time concentrating on those two questions and what was confusing for you."* Using the latter approach, it's likely we'd all be more inclined to listen to Mr. Valdez.

Activity

4.4 Examine the lesson plan below. Think about how you might adjust your teaching if you discover that your students did not meet the objectives and develop a reteaching lesson.

Lesson Plan

Subject: ___Science_____   Date _____

Objective: The student will: (1) describe the Mesozoic Era's climate, life forms, and continental shapes. (2) develop a time line showing the three periods from earliest to latest with animal and plant features in each period.

What prior knowledge/skills do students need? Some history of the Earth

How will student mastery be determined? Class Q & A and timeline

Materials: Textbook and adding machine tape

Teacher Actions	Student Actions
Bellwork: Describe Earth 250 million years ago. **Introduction** Ask students to read aloud their descriptions Introduce the Lesson Ask: *What do you know about Earth's history?* *How old is Earth?* *When did dinosaurs live?*	Students respond in journal Pair Share Students orally respond
Presenting the Lesson Present terms: Mesozoic Era, Triassic, Jurassic, Cretaceous, Pangea Direct students to read text. Q & A Discuss with class questions at end of text section on Mesozoic Era. Give adding machine tape and direct students to make a timeline of Mesozoic Era including animals and plants of the era.	Students write terms in notebook and define using text glossary. Students read silently. Students respond orally to questions Students make timeline
Closing the Lesson (review or wrap up) Ask: *How does this information fit with what you've seen in movies or on TV?* Collect timelines	Students respond.

During the Q & A, you noted that very few students responded to the questions. That evening, as you reviewed the timelines, you discover that the timelines are incomplete or inaccurate for the majority of the class. What will you do tomorrow so that students reach the objectives?

Why is monitoring and adjusting important? It allows you to correct learning mistakes immediately and prevents students from developing bad habits. I once taught a child who would add two-digit numbers by starting from the left column. No one apparently noticed nor corrected this bad habit, which was unfortunate when he started addition with regrouping.

> Never, if possible, lie down at night without being able to say: I have made one human being, at least, a little wiser, a little happier, or a little better this day. – Charles Kingsley

Monitoring and adjusting safeguards that you will teach to the correct level of difficulty. If we teach at a student's frustration level, very little learning occurs, so maintaining the correct instructional level is important.

Finally, the process of monitoring and adjusting increases the likelihood of student success and nothing ruins motivation like failure. If we target the learning at the instructional level, monitor progress and adjust when necessary, the likelihood that students will experience success will be high. Isn't this what we're about?

Five

To me the sole hope of
human salvation lies in
teaching.-George Bernard
Shaw

Assessing Learning

When we examined how to monitor student learning in Module 4, we looked at several formative methods. However, there comes a when we must assess our students' knowledge and skills. This type of assessment, which usually occurs at the end of the learning process, is called summative evaluation. We often associate the objective test for this purpose, but there are many ways to find out if, and what, our students have learned.

You might think that classroom assessment is necessary because of the current trend in accountability. Yes, that's partly true. Actually, classroom assessment is necessary so you can make informed decisions regarding student progress, instruction and curriculum. Imagine a classroom where your students are all smiling and enjoying the lesson. Their heads bobble up and down at everything you say. You think you're brilliant and that they understand everything. Unfortunately, your conclusions (being brilliant and students are learning) could be erroneous unless you check them out with some type of assessment.

Assessment also helps you determine the effectiveness of your teaching. Imagine your classroom again and half of your students did not demonstrate mastery on a particular concept or skill. You can blame the students for not studying or you can examine your teaching method. Maybe you just didn't spend enough time on that particular concept or skill. Maybe you didn't provide enough guided practice. Or, maybe, the test itself was at fault. The beauty of assessment is that it allows us to examine our curriculum, instruction, and evaluation methods to determine where and why we didn't get the learning results we desired.

Popham (2005) states that a large number of teachers view assessment as a method to assign grades. If we want grades to accurately reflect the student's progress on the learning outcomes/objectives, then the tests we use should accurately measure that progress. This means you need to develop or select tests that

a.) truly measure the course objectives,
b.) are fair, and
c.) are appropriate for the level of the student.

The more evidence we have of a student's learning, the more reliable the grades will be in accurately reflecting the student's progress. Imagine a parent questioning a grade you gave their child and you, not having any data to support the grade, saying, *I just didn't think he learned anything.*

Different Types of Assessments

Let's examine some of the different ways we can assess student learning. According to Stiggins (1997) there are four basic formats we can use to evaluate learning. The most common, and, perhaps overused, method is the selected response, or objective test. This is the multiple choice, matching, and/or true-false type where the student selects an answer from a number of choices (thus, the term selected response). In these assessments, students do not create an answer but identify the best answer from a list of choices.

A second type of classroom assessment is the essay test, or constructive response (Popham, 2005). This test ranges from the short answer where the student provides a few sentences to an extended response with multiple paragraphs. In essay assessments, students formulate and write the answer, thus, the student's ability to write is an integral factor in essay tests.

The third type is performance assessment. In this assessment, students do something. They may perform, as in singing or role playing, or they might produce a product, such as a brochure, poster, or research paper. Performance assessments may be completed in one class sitting or over several weeks. (More on this format later.)

The last type is the oral communication assessment. Teachers observe students during question-answer interactions, class discussions, student-teacher conferences, or even an oral examination. Though not as objective (in some cases) as other methods, it a very flexible means of assessment.

Assessment Targets

So how do you choose the best assessment method? You have to select the appropriate method for the specific learning objective(s). Stiggins states that different achievement "targets," or outcomes, require different types of assessment. For example, students learning about the geography, culture, and history of African countries, might complete a selected response test focusing on vocabulary and facts as well as complete a brochure on one country that examines its history, culture, resources, people, and current problems.

> Learning is never done without errors and defeat.-Vladimir Lenin

How we assess is directly tied to *what* we assess. Therefore, it is essential that you remain very clear about your objectives before you design or choose an assessment method. For example, your goal might be that you want your students to "know" how to use a ruler. Does this "knowing" mean that they will describe uses for a ruler, distinguish a 12" ruler from a yardstick, measure a line with a ½" ruler, or measure objects with the appropriate instrument (yardstick vs. ruler)? The more specific your objectives are, the better your instruction and assessment.

To identify what to assess, you need to ask four questions:

What do my students need to know and understand to meet the standard/objectives?
What reasoning patterns must they master?
What performance skills must the master?
What products must they be able to create?

Stiggins uses the term "target" to describe the different outcomes and classified typical assessment targets into five groups: Knowledge, Reasoning, Skill, Product, and Dispositions. Let's take a closer look at these targets.

Knowledge

Knowledge objectives include those we associate with Bloom's knowledge category which include the recall of facts, terms, basic concepts, and principles. Knowledge, however, without understanding, is insufficient and Stiggins includes objectives at Bloom's comprehension level in this target. Learning at this level would include explaining, illustrating, interpreting, summarizing, demonstrating, and classifying. In each of these objectives, the learner is asked to show they understand the facts and ideas. Also included in this target is the knowledge of procedures, such as how to locate longitude and latitude, or the steps in the writing process or scientific method.

Reasoning

Targets in the reasoning category include Bloom's Application, Analysis and Evaluation levels. At these levels, students are required to use information. Students might solve a math problem, analyze a story, apply the scientific method, compare two countries, or present support in a persuasive argument.

Skill

There are many skills which teachers encourage such as cooperative work skills, oral reading fluency, or science lab safety. Often, these types of skills require the learner to have both knowledge of facts/concepts and procedures, and the application of these procedures. Notice that a skill such as *Using the Internet*, requires the learner to operate a computer, know what the Internet is, and understand how to access the Internet, just to begin. Even the elementary skill of writing the letters of the alphabet is a complex combination of knowledge of letters, how to hold a pencil, and the procedure for forming each letter. These types of assessments usually have accompanying rubrics.

Product

In the creation of a product, the learner must have acquired the three previous targets. For example, if a student conducts a science experiment (performance) and writes a lab report (product), he/she must have concept and procedural knowledge, reasoning skills to form conclusions and hypotheses, and skills in manipulating equipment. Children who produce a brochure on a country have knowledge and comprehension of facts and concepts, demonstrate skill in researching, and display skill in writing. This type of assessment also has an accompanying rubric.

Dispositions/Attitudes

Stiggins defines the category of dispositions as targets that go beyond the academic area and include attitudes toward something, interest in something, or personal areas such as self-concept and self-efficacy. These areas are rarely assessed. While they are important to the development of each student, objective assessment is very difficult. To illustrate, a group of teachers wanted to increase their students' self-concepts. When asked how they intended to measure this, they considered counting how many times the children smiled.

Besides the fact that the method would have been cumbersome, teachers realized that smiling is not necessarily an indicator of positive self-concept. Assessment of dispositions requires a clear definition of very complex factors and, as such, we will not deal with this target here.

Activity

5.1 Consider your subject area(s). Examine a unit you will be teaching and categorize the outcomes according to Stiggins' target organization.

Grade/Unit: _____

Category	Outcome (s)
Knowledge	
Reasoning	
Skill	
Product	
Disposition	

Matching outcomes and methods

Probably the easiest way to match assessment with learning outcomes (objectives) is to create a chart that lists the objectives and assessment methods. If you create a chart that links your objectives to the appropriate assessment method, you can see that there are many ways to assess a single objective. On the following page, we will examine the objectives and possible assessments for a poetry unit.

Poetry Unit

Objective (Target) The student will:	Selected Response	Essay	Performance	Oral Communication
Knowledge: a. define poetry terms b. identify figurative language in poems	Multiple choice and matching on terms and figurative language	Essay on one poem focusing on figurative language	Write a poem using examples of each figurative term Notebook/journal	Class discussion; Question-Answer interaction
Reasoning a. summarize the meaning of a poem b. compare two poems on meaning, and structure c. evaluate a poem		Essays on several poems	Poster Oral presentation Poetry notebook	Class discussion: Question-Answer interaction
Skills a. write poems using particular structures or styles b. create an anthology of poems on a theme.			Create own poems Anthology	
Attitudes/Dispositions a. show an interest in poetry b. demonstrate a willingness to read poetry	Answers a rating scale on poetry	Open-ended questionnaire	Teacher Observation	Interview

Will you conduct ALL these assessments? In a perfect world…no, not even then. One selected-response assessment, however, may not be sufficient to determine mastery of all the objectives. Certainly using all the methods listed on the chart would be overwhelming and, in some cases, redundant. Your task is to select the most efficient methods to determine if your students have mastered the learning objectives.

Here's an example of objectives and possible assessment from a math unit:

Outcome The student will:	Selected Response	Essay	Performance	Personal Communication
Knowledge -recognize angle relationships -define terms	Multiple Choice		Tri-fold brochure Notebook	Class Q & A
Reasoning a. -solve ratio problems b. -calculate volume of complex figures c. - calculate area and arc length of circles	Fill in the Blank ratio problems		Solve ratio problems Solve volume problems Solve circle problems	
Skill -explain the steps in solving volume problems		Write the steps solving the volume of a cube	Mini-poster	

It should be apparent to you that good assessment, just like effective instruction, begins with a clearly stated objective. If you want your students to solve ratio problems, then the assessment must match the objective and students should be given a sufficient number of problems to solve in order to demonstrate mastery. It would not be appropriate to ask students to identify ratio problems from a list if you're measuring their ability to "solve." The student's actions on an assessment must match the intended learning outcome.

Activity

5.2 Look at the objectives below taken from a social studies curriculum. Determine different assessments, as in the previous examples, for each outcome.

Outcome The student will:	Selected Response	Essay	Performance	Personal Communication
Locate on maps and globes their local community, state, the United States, the seven continents, and the four oceans.				
Construct a country map, using cardinal directions (N,S,E,W)and map symbols.				
Describe how location, weather, and physical environment affect the way people live, including the effects on their food, clothing, shelter, transportation, and recreation.				

> We must be clear thinkers, capable of communicating effectively both to those being assessed and to those who must understand the assessment's results. – R. Stiggins

Something else you may have noticed is that one objective may be assessed using different formats. Here's an example from science:

Objective: Students will recognize general properties of solutions and suspensions.

Selected Response
Which of the following is a property of a solution?
    a. prevents postoperative shock
    b. is heterogeneous
    c. does not pass through membranes
    d. is clear

Essay
List at least 3 properties of a solution and three properties of a suspension.

Product/Performance

Prepare 2 examples of a solution and 2 examples of a suspension. Be prepared to explain the properties of each example which make it either a solution or suspension.

Here's another example from a novel study on *To Kill a Mockingbird* by Harper Lee

Objective: Students will describe the setting of a story.

Essay
What kind of town is Maycomb, Alabama? In your answer, discuss the economic and educational levels of the town's people and the societal views given the time period of the story. Use information from the story and class discussion.

Personal Communication
Compare and contrast Maycomb to our city in at least three different ways.

Product/Performance
Draw a map of Maycomb, Alabama. Be sure to use information from the story to create the details in your map.

So which test method do you choose? The essential question is: *Does the assessment match the learning outcome in an adequate manner?* If it does, then you must consider time constraints—Is there time available in class and out-of-class for test preparation, administration, and scoring?

When do you plan assessments?

Ineffective teachers may get to the end of a unit and decide it's time for a test. Others may decide they need more data to determine a grade and announce a test for the end of the week. And a few contemplate testing their students on their drive to work. Effective teachers consider their assessments before they begin their unit. In fact, the best thing to do is to concurrently plan your assessments as you plan your unit. After all, planning your assessments when you organize your learning objectives just makes good sense! You should make a chart, similar to the previous examples, which outlines the objectives along with the possible assessment formats.

Activity

5.3 Create your own matrix that includes the objectives for a unit of study and the method(s) of assessment you might use.

Outcome The student will:	Selected Response	Essay	Performance	Personal Communication

Developing the Assessment

So how do you actually write a test? Most curricular materials today provide ready-made tests that correspond to the curriculum. These assessment materials include selected response-type items as well as essays and performance tasks (alternative assessments). This is the place to start. Don't be too eager to use the accompanying tests in their printed form, however. You should always examine these prepared tests for the following (Airasian, 2007):

1.   Do the test questions cover the objectives taught and emphasized?

In some cases, you may not have sufficiently covered the objectives specified in the text or you may have added your own objectives. The prepared test might also include items on material that you did not teach at all. In these cases, you might have to edit the existing test by eliminating items or adding additional test questions to assess objectives on which you did focus.

2. Do the test questions use vocabulary familiar to your students'?

Sometimes, the authors of the test questions use vocabulary that is unfamiliar to your students and that may interfere with their ability to answer the question correctly. Recently, while reviewing a test, a teacher was heard saying, "You needed to know what *comparative advantage* meant to answer this question." You don't want to explain vocabulary used in the test item *after* the test is given. If possible, change the vocabulary in the test to match your language, as those are the words with which students can identify. If the test software doesn't allow you to edit test items, be sure to go over the unfamiliar vocabulary before students begin the test.

3. Do the test questions require your students to perform the behaviors that you taught?

If you taught students to locate places on a map, then don't ask students to draw a map on the test. There should be a one-to-one correlation between the learning objective, what you required your students to do in class and what they are asked to do on the test.

4. Are there a sufficient number of test items to judge pupil performance?

How many test items is "sufficient?" This one is tricky. Clearly, one or two questions may not be enough to reliably measure student learning, and 100 items are probably too many. The number of items depends on your students' ages, levels of ability, and the time available for the test. The assessment of learning targets using different assessment methods can help lesson the need for a large number of selected response items.

5. If the assessment requires a skill or product, is there an accompanying rubric?

It is always wise to provide the rubric along with the directions for any performance assessment. You want to ensure that the evaluative criteria match your objective(s) and are described in such as manner so that both you and your students understand them.

If there isn't a prepared rubric, you will need to develop one.

> The best teachers are those that tell you where to look but don't tell you what to see.- Alexandra Trenfor

If the test provided with your curricula materials matches your objectives and the way you taught the material, then using prepared tests can save you a lot of time. Test bank software now accompanies many curricula materials. This software is really helpful as you can select test items from a bank of questions, edit existing questions and add your own. If you have access to this type of software, it's the easiest way to create a custom test while keeping your learning objectives uppermost in your planning. Just remember to evaluate each question in the bank on its vocabulary and target objective before you select it.

But what if you don't have assessment materials or computer software? Making a good, valid test takes time so you shouldn't start the night before test day! There are some excellent texts on test construction. Here are four:

Carey L. M. (2001). *Measuring and Evaluating School Learning*, 4th ed. Needham Heights, MA: Allyn and Bacon

Popham, W. J. (2007). *Classroom Assessment: What Teachers Need to Know*, 5th ed. Needham Heights, MA: Allyn and Bacon.

Stiggins, R. (1997). *Student Centered Classroom Assessment, 2nd ed.* NY: Macmillan Pub. Co.

Wiggins, G. (1998). *Educative Assessment: Designing Assessments to Inform and Improve Student Performance* . San Francisco, Calif: Jossey-Bass.

Whether you use a commercially prepared test, select items from a software test bank, or create your own test items, be sure to take the time to proofread the final product before you hand it out to students. Measuring student learning should not be hindered by unfamiliar vocabulary, misspellings, and/or poor grammar on test items.

Developing Performance Assessments and Rubrics

Performance assessment requires students to demonstrate what they know or can do through the development of a product or an actual performance. These assessments can provide clear evidence of students' achievements and are useful for a wide range of classroom activities, including essays, science projects, public speaking, and multimedia projects.

Teachers often use performance tasks as culminating activities at the end of an instructional unit, but these tasks can be integrated at any time in the learning. One of the unique characteristics of performance assessment is that it is frequently indistinguishable from instruction. Performance tasks should be considered an integral part of the learning and not as "add-ons" at the end of a unit of instruction.

In general, performance assessments fall into one of the categories listed below:

1. Short performance tasks – These are task which are open-ended and can be completed within a class time period or less. Examples include completing graphic organizers, journal writing, graphing data, completing a map, math problem solving, making a scientific drawing, or creating a time line.
2. Event tasks – With these tasks, students usually engage in some type of event, such as viewing, reading, or completing a unit. These may be completed in one-three class segments. Examples include responding to literature by creating a book jacket, conducting a science experiment and writing a lab report, developing a geographic picture dictionary, writing a myth (short story, poem, etc.), creating a pamphlet, or making a healthy snack.
3. Extended Tasks –Activities that take longer than one week and are considered "projects" fall into this category. These tasks may required work outside of class in

the form of research and might be polished products for audiences in and outside of the classroom. Examples include: creating a power point on a research topic, developing a TV documentary script on an historical figure, planning and growing a community garden, science experiment, writing a research report, or maintaining a portfolio.

Performance tasks usually have more than one acceptable solution and can tap the higher cognitive levels of Bloom's taxonomy. For example, when students are asked to solve a community problem, the student must research alternative solutions, create a response to the problem and then explain or defend it. This process involves the use of higher-order thinking skills, such as, analysis, reasoning, and problem solving.

To design a performance assessment task you must begin with the identification of outcomes that accompany your course curriculum. For example, the following outcomes clearly require assessments other than selective response formats:

- Summarizes narrative or expository writings.
- Explains significant developments and extinctions of plant and animal life on the geologic time scale.
- Compares and contrasts two works of art made by the use of different art tools and media
- Constructs, interprets, and uses scale drawings
- Writes a persuasive essay

You must ask yourself several important questions in the development phase:

1. What concept, skill, or knowledge am I trying to assess?
2. What should my students know?
3. At what level should my students be performing?
4. What type of knowledge is being assessed: reasoning, skill, disposition, or product?

By answering these questions, you can decide what type of activity best suits your assessment needs. Once the outcomes are defined, the next step is to create a task that will allow the students to demonstrate their knowledge, reasoning, skills, and/or attitudes. These tasks should be authentic (real-world), feasible (in time, space, and cost), fair (not biased based on gender, race, etc.), flexible (allow multiple outcomes), and observable. Assessment tasks can relate to real-life experiences, make connections to personal experiences, and require demonstrations of competency and mastery. Ideas for assessment tasks can come from the text, your curriculum, current events, literature, the arts, reference books, and the Internet.

Examples:

essays	power point	models	travel brochure
autobiography	oral report	poster	business letter
drawing or illustrations	notebook	research report	venn diagram

What Makes a Performance Assessment?

Performance assessments are composed of 3 distinct parts: a performance task description (scenario), a format in which the student responds, and a predetermined scoring system (rubric). As you develop your task, think about the end product. Ask yourself, *What would the perfect finished product or performance look like?* Once you have that vision, create a scenario to prompt your students.

One of the most important considerations in developing your task is the interest level of your students. You might create a unique performance task for your poetry unit, but if your students think it's "dumb" or just "busy work," the results may be less than what you expected. Writing a book report is considered a performance task, yet, student response to the task might be lukewarm if you don't make it more interesting by adding a creative twist. Students are often asked to compare different forms of government but how about asking them to generate a government for a new country? Student interest is a key factor in the success or failure of your performance assessment.

Another consideration is the amount of structure you will provide to students. You might specifically define the problem or simply state, "*Find a community problem.*" You may give students comprehensive information on what needs to be contained in the final product, or you might tell them to decide for themselves how they will present their findings.

> As schools continue to evolve, we will come to rely on performance assessment as part of the basis for our evaluation of student achievement. - R. Stiggins

Consider the following example:

Your club needs $100.00 to go on a field trip. The members have decided to hold a fundraiser but don't know what to do. Your group's task is to determine a product for your fundraiser, the costs to you, the cost to your consumer, and the amount of product you need to sell to make your desired profit.

You will present your ideas to the class in any form your group selects.

In this activity, the problem and the content of the product are highly defined, but the solution choices and manner in which group responds is left open.

Activity

5.4 Rewrite the following performance tasks to create a higher level of structure:

Task	New scenario
1. Write a song.	
2. Develop a question, conduct a survey, and analyze your results.	
3. Identify an issue at our school and write a letter to the principal with your ideas.	

5.6 Choose one of the outcomes from your content area that can be evaluated through a performance task. Write a performance task scenario to measure that outcome.

Rubrics

Once you have created the task, you will need to make the assessment criteria, usually in the form of a rubric. Performance-based assessments may not have clear-cut right or wrong answers. Rather, there are degrees to which a person is successful or unsuccessful. Thus, in creating your rubric, you need to define "success." A rubric is a rating system which allows you to determine the quality of a product and/or at what level of proficiency a student is able to perform a task.

Effective assessment criteria clearly communicate to students the standards of achievement that you expect. In developing your rubric, you must specify all the key elements needed for success and define a continuum for each element. For example, a brochure's key elements may include organization, evidence of research, accuracy, neatness, creativity, and writing conventions (grammar, spelling etc.). The continuum might be a number indicating some degree (see below) or a term, such as *weak, adequate, or strong.*

There are three basic categories of rubrics for performance assessment: checklists, rating scales, and holistic scoring. Each type of rubric has advantages, disadvantages, and appropriate applications for classrooms. Below at an example of a rating scale rubric used to evaluate a student's notebook.

	4	3	2	1	Your Points
Completion of Notebook sections	All required sections are complete	One required section is missing	2-3 sections are missing	More than 3 sections are missing	
Organization	All assignments and notes are kept in a logical sequence.	One or two assignments and notes are not in a logical sequence.	3-4 assignments and notes are not in a logical sequence.	More than 4 assignments and notes are not in a logical sequence.	
Neatness	Notebook is neat and orderly. Papers are secured, and notebook is clean.	Notebook is kept in a satisfactory condition. Some papers may not be secured.	Notebook is not kept in a satisfactory condition. Papers are not secured, pages may be wrinkled and dirty.	Notebook is unkept, soiled, and generally untidy.	

There are numerous Internet sources that can provide you with ready-made rubrics or with the technology to create your own rubric. Here are just a few sites:

www.teach-nology.com/web_tools/rubrics
www.rubrics4teachers.com
www.intranet.cps.k12.il.us/assessments_and_Rubrics/Rubric_Bank/rubric_bank.html
school.discoveryeducation.com/schrockguide/assess.html

For a thorough treatment on the development of performance tasks and rubrics, see
Stiggins, R. J. (1997) *Student-Centered Classroom Assessment*, 2nd ed.

Activity

5.7 Create a rubric to accompany the performance task you developed previously.

General Preparation and Administration of Tests

Planning and developing good tests is not enough for the fair, accurate assessment of student learning. Effective teachers know how to prepare students for the test and how to administer those tests.

Have you ever had a teacher yell out at the end of class, "Test Friday!" You might have had several questions, such as, On what material? How many questions? What type of questions? etc. Effective teachers prepare their students for tests by orienting them to the purpose of the test, the content covered in the test, the format of the test, and how the test results will be used (Szafran, 1981; Barger, 1983).

Here's an example of how to appropriately orient your students to a test:

We will complete the section on the skeletal system today and will have a short multiple choice test on the chapter on Friday. This test will cover mainly vocabulary from that chapter and will include two short essay questions from the section review that you completed for homework. This test grade will count toward your final grade.

It's a good idea to also write the test date and test contents on the board for any students who were absent the day of your announcement. This type of preparation may decrease test anxiety and increase test achievement. If you have a calendar or web site or use some type of Internet connection for parents announcing homework, be sure to publicize test dates there as well.

On test day, it is important that you set the tone by arranging the physical setting. Make sure the desks are spaced to discourage cheating and that your test copies are correctly collated and ready to distribute. You want to make your classroom environment as favorable as possible which includes keeping the classroom at a comfortable room temperature, ensuring there is adequate lighting,

> Fundamentally, educational assessment rests on a foundation of common sense. –W. J. Popham

76

and decreasing distractions, such as noise.

When you give out the test don't just hand it out and walk away. It's important to review the directions and format of the test. For example, *Let's read the general directions... The first 15 questions are multiple choice, the next section is true-false, and the last is an essay question based on your lab work.* If there are any words that you think might pose a problem, you should review them before the test begins. At this point, you need to tell students the procedure when they finish: *When you are done with the test, fold it in half and raise your hand. I will come pick it up. You may then read silently until everyone is finished.* Your final words should be encouraging: *Everyone should do well on this test because you've been working hard. If you have questions, please raise your hand and I'll come to your desk. Good luck.* If you are positive and encouraging, then students will perceive that they have an opportunity to be successful on the test (Moore & Davies, 1984; Kirkland, 1971).

It's tempting to sit down and relax while your students take their test, but don't! This is the time to move about and monitor student behavior. Your active monitoring of the test communicates to students that this is important. Monitoring by walking around does discourage cheating but also allows you to observe students who might have difficulty getting started. If a student doesn't have a pencil/pen, provide it without disturbing those nearby. If a student seems confused, you can answer his/her questions quietly. This is not the time to reprimand students for not being prepared!

Observing students also lets you know how long they are taking to complete the test. Student performance should not be dependent on speed (unless it's a typing test). As the end time nears, you should observe if a large number of students are still working and need more time. Generally speaking, a longer test will give you more accurate scores but shouldn't be so long that the majority of your students do not finish. Your test time limits should be generous enough for 90% of your students to complete all the questions.

Now consider a test that's too short. If all your students finish the test in 20 minutes what will you and your students do for the rest of the time period? If you're not monitoring, students with large blocks of unstructured idle time could develop into management problems. In planning your assessment, you must prepare some type of quiet activity for those who finish early, i.e. word search, crossword puzzle, independent reading. By carefully monitoring the administration of the test, you will increase the likelihood that optimal test conditions are maintained for all your students.

What to do with test results

The reason for summative testing is to make decisions regarding student achievement. So while the data is informative for you, it is also helpful to students. Effective teachers examine test data and give feedback to their students regarding their performance.

The most common way to express student performance on a classroom test is to use the percent correct. This is determined by dividing the number correct by the total questions on the test. A student who correctly answered seven out of ten questions would have a 70% correct. Once you have all students' percent correct scores, you need to ask yourself some questions:

1. Was there a question(s) that many students missed? If so, you need to find out why and may consider discounting the item(s).
2. What percent of students scored a 70% correct or higher? As 70% is considered a passing grade and a mark for mastery, if most of your students fell into this range, you can safely assume they met the objective(s). If, however, a large number of your students did not meet the 70% correct criterion, then you need to consider some options:
   a. Reteach the entire material
   b. Reteach selected areas
   c. Provide remediation only to students who didn't demonstrate mastery
   d. Discount the test and try again at a later date

When students perform poorly on a test, one can hear teachers blame the students for not studying, not trying, or not caring. In truth, we need to consider two other alternatives. It is possible that the test was not a fair assessment. It is also possible that we just didn't do a good job of teaching the material. The one thing we don't want to do is publicly chastise our students for doing a poor job or for not studying when we return their tests.

Activity

5.8 What would you do or say if these were your class test results? Write your response:

1. The class mean on the literature test was 80%. However, on the question examining the author's purpose, 85% of the class answered it incorrectly.

2. The class completed a unit on ecosystems and you gave a 20 item multiple-choice test. The class mean was 72%. You noticed a large number of students confused terms such as habitat, niche, and ecosystem.

3. On a test covering map symbols, the class mean was 85%. Only two students scored below a 70% correct.

Remember that a summative test is designed to tell you if students did not master a particular objective. So, if you find that a student didn't meet the objective, you must provide remedial instruction. If you do not remediate, you risk negatively impacting future learning and motivation.

Feedback to Students

Giving feedback to students can impact student achievement and increase student learning. A student once recounted how he had worked hard on a project, and, one day, three weeks later, his teacher passed his desk and, nonchalantly said, "Oh, you made a B on your paper." He said he didn't work as hard on the next project.

Feedback is provided by you to students regarding their performance and answers questions such as: How am I doing? What do I need to do better? Feedback is not praise or blame but is value-neutral. It describes what the child did and did not do. (Wiggins, 1998). Teachers who pass back a test or project and do not take the time to discuss it miss a great opportunity for reinforcing learning and reducing misunderstandings. Research tells us that for feedback to impact learning it must be specific to student work and it must be timely. (Lysakowski & Walbert, 1981)

> The only person who is educated is the one who has learned how to learn and change. -- Carl Rogers

The type of feedback we give should be instructional and nonjudgmental. Providing a number correct or a percentage score along with some specific comment is more effective than just writing a grade or number correct alone. Comments such as *Good work*, or *Your answer shows thought* are nice but not instructive. The more specific your comment regarding the student's answer, the stronger the likelihood for improved achievement. (Bangert-Drowns, Kulik, Kulik, & Morgan, 1991)Your comment should explain where and why the student made an error. *You confused cerebellum and cerebrum in your answer*, or *You didn't apply the rule for order of operations.* You should balance your comments with suggestions on how to improve as well as comments on what the student did correctly. Elawar and Corno (1985) proposed four questions to guide your feedback: **What is the key error? What is the probable reason the student made this error? How can I guide the student to avoid the error? What did the student do well that can be noted?**

Feedback should be given in a factual way without passing judgment on your students. For example, *The average for this class on the test was 82%. It seemed you all had problems with question number 5 so let's look at that one.* Saying to your students, *What were you thinking? You must not have been paying attention when I went over that*, is <u>not</u> a good feedback strategy.

Some teachers will caution you to stay away from red pens and use another ink color to mark papers. It's not the color of the ink but the way in which you mark the paper. Do you make a big X on incorrect answers or do you place a check mark next to the correct ones? Do you write a -10 at the top or do you put a +60? Do you draw a sad face or do you make an encouraging comment? If we make negative comments using purple ink, students will come to feel about purple the way they do about red.

When you return their tests, you want to review the questions on which students seemed to have difficulty. Go over the answers and the rational for those answers. Where possible, point out the answers in the text. Take this opportunity to clarify any misconceptions or errors in thinking. If you used a performance assessment, be sure to go over the rubric and allow students to examine where they fell short on the criteria for success. Planning time for feedback is just as important as planning the test itself.

The timing of your feedback on a test may be significant. Some researchers have found that waiting at least 24 hours after a test to give feedback may increase future achievement. Other studies have found immediate feedback on classroom quizzes was more effective than delayed feedback. It is safe to conclude that feedback is important and should be offered in a timely manner. In general, tests should be returned within two days of their administration. The longer the delay in providing feedback, the less impact the feedback has on learning.

Activity

5.9 Practice making encouraging statements below. For each situation, write a brief positive feedback comment you might use on the student's test paper.

Situation	Your feedback comment
Jesse made his first 100% correct on a spelling test.	
Mandy attempted 15 items and correctly answered 10 of those but didn't finish the test which had 20 items. Her grade was a 50%.	
Juan used the wrong formula for finding the area of a triangle but he used the other area formulas correctly. He scored a 75%.	
Lindsay scored a 70% because she didn't answer any questions on the second page.	

Some final thoughts...

Did your teachers ever require you to get your parent's signature on your test paper? This is a method some teachers use to communicate with parents about their child's progress. If you ask students to get a parent signature, remember that you have to check for this the following day which takes time away from instruction. If students don't get a parent signature, then you have to be prepared to follow through with some consequence.

Communicating with parents is critical and there are numerous ways to accomplish this. Most teachers provide parents with written information on their homework and grading policies. During the year, you can send notes home, provide periodic progress reports, develop a homework website, create a newsletter with the students, and, of course, invite parents to conferences. Whatever the age of the student, you must develop a plan for communicating with their parent or guardian.

Unless it's a secure test, it's a mystery why teachers do not allow students to keep their test papers. You remember those teachers? They passed out the test, let you look over your score and answers, and then took the tests back up. Test papers should be considered instructional materials and students should be allowed to keep them in their notebooks.

Confidentiality

The Buckley Amendment of 1974 states that all educational agencies must make test results available to students and/or their parents. This means that the information should be reliable and valid and any written statements must be based on defensible evidence. If you include comments or anecdotes in cumulative folders, observation forms, report cards, or other communications, these should be accurate, factual, and fair.

Because of confidentially issues, you cannot publicly post test scores or grades anywhere using student names or their student numbers if in alphabetical order. What is the best approach? You, (not a student), should return test papers, keep the results confidential, and inform parents through progress reports, scholarship warnings, or calls home if their child is not progressing. Finally, don't forget to record the test grades in your grade book.

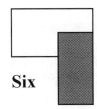

Six

If people are good only because they fear punishment, and hope for reward, then we are a sorry lot indeed.-Albert Einstein

Classroom Management-Focusing on Prevention

Mario is asleep at his desk. Jenna and Donna are passing notes. Scott is daydreaming during seatwork. Lydia is packing her books with 10 minutes left in the period and Brian is drawing cartoons instead of working on his assignment. If you were a visitor to this classroom, you might ask, *"Who's in charge?"*

One of the major areas of concern for teachers, principals, and parents is the management of student behavior in the classroom. The term "classroom management" is thought by some to refer only to student behavior, or to be synonymous with control; however, management is a much broader term that encompasses everything concerning the classroom environment and how teachers maximize the time allotted for learning. Management is about how we increase the opportunities for learning while decreasing the disruptions to learning. *Discipline* is the term that refers to the prevention of and response to student misbehavior.

You will find that effective teachers usually have a comprehensive approach to the prevention of misbehavior when they create their management plan. They consider the classroom learning environment and how they can establish an environment conducive to learning before they ever meet their students. Such a management plan would include how to present content, or curriculum, how to develop classroom relationships, and how to create and maintain standards for behavior.

There's no doubt that effective teachers have an impact on student learning. Research reported Marzano's *Classroom Management that Works* (2003) shows that students of effective classroom managers can demonstrate achievement gains of about 52 percentile points while those of ineffective teachers might only gain 14 percentile points. Marzano also reported that teachers who utilized "disciplinary interventions" had substantially fewer classroom disruptions. This makes sense, doesn't it? If you have to deal less with behavior problems and interruptions, then you will maximize the time allocated for learning and, thus, students will ultimately demonstrate increased achievement.

> Classroom management: *all the strategies and methods teachers use to successfully complete the learning goal.*

You should think about classroom management in a more comprehensive framework than just discipline or control. With this expanded meaning, dealing with behavior "problems" is only one component of classroom management. Whole books and college courses have been devoted to the concept of classroom management; therefore, it would be impracticable to present the entire body of knowledge here. However, the ideas that follow will get you on track toward a successful beginning.

Who Are Effective Managers?

So what does an effective classroom teacher actually do? Like all managers, the teacher is the one who plans, organizes, directs, coordinates, guides and cares about his/her students. Some people think managing is about compliance- getting people to do what you want even if they don't want to. In a compliance-oriented classroom, students do things because they are told to. This type of classroom requires a firm and rigid set of rules and consequences, and the teacher usually relies on aggressive and/or hostile methods of implementation.

Try to remember the last time you were under an authoritarian leader. Was it a comfortable environment to be in? Usually, you didn't have any input into what happened and may have been treated with little or no respect. Under these conditions, some people become defiant and hostile toward the leader. And, while some may be compliant, they are not at ease. Students also might indeed behave in a compliance-oriented classroom, but they wouldn't necessarily be cooperative about the primary goal of the class, which is learning.

Managing is more about getting students' *cooperation* than about making them obey you and a set of rules. Managing is about developing students' self-reliance, responsibility and thinking skills. Your first question, before you ever see your students, is: *Do I want to focus on managing or controlling?*

> A master can tell you what he expects of you. A teacher, though, awakens your own expectations. – Patricia Neal

What type of planning is necessary?

Effective classroom managers plan their room arrangement, classroom rules, consequences for misbehavior, how they will respond to inappropriate behavior, monitoring devices, and reward systems. Research shows that effective teachers work on rules and procedures in the first three weeks of the school year but also emphasize socialization and group dynamics. According to Borich (2006) effective classroom managers demonstrate three broad areas of good teaching: extensive planning and organizing of the room, methodical teaching of rules and routines, and informing students about the consequences of breaking rules and applying consequences consistently.

Warmth vs. Control

Classroom management planning also includes decisions regarding your classroom climate. We can think about climate as a combination of control and warmth. In a classroom designed around high levels of teacher control and very little warmth, the classroom climate might be motivated by fear. Teachers may shout, threaten, glare at students and even use sarcasm. In this classroom, student compliance leads to feelings of helplessness and may manifest itself in power struggles with the teacher, other students, and/or the school. Classrooms high in teacher warmth but low in control may be characterized as highly permissive and students may have lots of freedom in choosing their behavior. Teachers in these classrooms may be unassertive, whiny, pleading with students, and apologetic. This type of classroom leads to student confusion and possibly chaos. Obviously, a climate that has moderate amounts of teacher control and warmth is the best possible situation.

Classrooms, which exercise the authoritarian forms of management with rigid rules, are considered passé. Given today's student characteristics, the best management technique is to develop student responsibility and, in the long run, foster a warmer classroom climate.

Experts advocate equal amounts of warmth and control. In this type of classroom, the

> One looks back with appreciation to the brilliant teachers, but with gratitude to those who touched our human feelings.-Carl Jung

teacher is assertive but not threatening. The teacher maintains eye contact and clearly states the expected behavior. On occasion, this teacher may raise his/her voice, but it is usually an appropriate volume to gain and focus student behavior. Students behave in this classroom because rules are well defined and consequences are consistently and fairly applied.

Activity

6.1 Think about your favorite classes in school. Can you describe the climate of those classes? What was the teacher like? Now visualize your classroom. Write a description of your class that includes the climate and how you see yourself with your students.

Components of Classroom Management

Let's examine the components of classroom management.

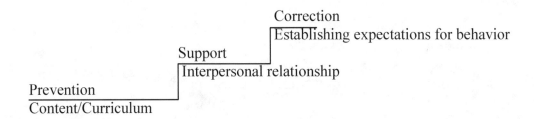

Correction
Establishing expectations for behavior
Support
Interpersonal relationship
Prevention
Content/Curriculum

Notice that the foundation of management is *prevention*. Be proactive. Dedicate yourself to preventing problems. As part of prevention, a good manager establishes a supportive environmental climate conducive to learning. Lastly, pro-active teachers establish boundaries for appropriate and acceptable behavior and consequences for misbehavior. When teachers emphasize the prevention and support aspects of their classrooms, they deal less often with correcting misconduct.

The chart below provides a brief overview of management strategies for each component (Shearer, 1997).

	Preventive Strategies	Supportive Strategies	Corrective Strategies
Content/Curriculum	• Planning Lessons • Using active learning • Aiming lessons at students' instructional level • Organizing time & materials • Connecting to students' prior knowledge	• Encouraging effort • Allowing students to contribute to the learning • De-emphasizing competition • Recognizing and rewarding progress and mastery • Making learning visible	• Providing specific feedback through monitoring • Adjusting instruction when necessary • Conferencing with student/parent about progress • Developing goals with the student
Interpersonal Relationships (Climate)	• Modeling respect: "please," "thank you," etc. • Learning students' names • Showing interest in students' outside activities • Developing a safe environment	• Using cooperative groups • Teaching social skills • Developing "I Can" attitude in students • Sending positive messages home	• Using class meetings • Conferencing with student and/or parent • Reminding and reteaching social skills
Expectations for Behavior	• Teaching & reteaching procedures • Creating and communicating rules and expectations	• Giving students voice • Providing recognition for positive behaviors • Conferencing with student and/or parent	• Using language of choice • Using assertive communication • Applying consequences fairly

Let's take a closer look at content and climate strategies.

Content /Curriculum: Preventive and Supportive Strategies

The greatest preventative technique is effective lesson planning. Lessons that engage students' interest and get students to actively participate in their learning will prevent most behavior problems. The aspects of effective lesson planning were examined in Chapters 2 and 3. But good lesson planning also includes: having your materials ready, anticipating problems, using a variety of teaching techniques, and showing your enthusiasm and passion for your subject. Sounds logical? Let's peek into Mr. Cook's class: Mr. Cook had his bellwork on the board, reviewed it with the class, introduced the day's topic, went over the reading and started distributing the handouts. Suddenly, a student says, *We did this one all ready, Mr. Cook!* Sure enough, Mr. Cook copied the wrong handout. The class begins to murmur and suddenly no one is focused on the learning. Even if Mr. Cook manages to find a new assignment, he has lost control of his class. Lost learning time is ineffective management.

Feelings of Success

Good lesson planning also means your students will feel successful, or at minimum, feel they can be successful. You can create success-oriented attitudes by gearing the lesson to the students' instructional level. If you have a diverse population in your classroom, you'll need to consider differentiating your lessons to meet the skill level of all the learners. Incorporating active learning and the different modalities into your lessons will increase student motivation and decrease opportunities for misbehavior.

It's also important for your students to feel they are a part of the lesson. To do this, you need to allow them to contribute ideas. This doesn't mean you're going to let them tell you what to teach. Think about incorporating more active learning strategies. If you find yourself talking all the time and answering your own questions, take a step back. Develop questions for your students to answer, write them down in your lesson plan, and use wait time. If you want to increase student involvement, you need to talk less.

If you give students feedback on their progress, their motivation will be higher. Don't you need encouragement on your performance? Students do too! Return student papers in a timely manner and write comments on the paper, not just the number right and a grade. You can give feedback informally as you walk around the room. Comment on their work with statements such as, *I like that opening paragraph; Your lab conclusion shows you understand the concept of osmosis;* or *You start out correctly but you need to reexamine the last two steps in solving the equation.*

> Education…is a painful, continual and difficult work to be done in kindness, by watching, by warning,…by praise, but above all-by example.-John Ruskin

Encouraging Effort

When children attribute their lack of success to their lack of ability, they may choose not to even try. Don't try = don't fail. Weiner (1978) found children who credited their failure to lack of ability eventually responded with resignation and apathy. All is not lost, however. Children can be taught to see their failure as a result of insufficient effort rather than their lack of ability and, eventually, increase their level of persistence. (Dweck, 1975). Our job as teachers, then, is to make students see the connection between effort and success.

If you develop lessons at students' instructional level, they will perceive the academic task as manageable and engage in the learning. In classrooms with multiple instructional levels, it is not always possible to individualize instruction so it will be up to you to use encouraging statements that focus on effort. Encouragement is nonjudgmental and focused on the task, process, product or behavior. Here are some examples:
Your work is showing definite improvement. Your efforts are paying off.
You're off to a good start with this introduction. Keep going.
You show real effort in the first two problems. Keep at it.

Another way teachers discourage children is by using competition. In classrooms that use competition for grades and awards, students who view themselves as less able than their peers will often show little or no effort. When teachers grade on the curve or post students' grades, they are spotlighting the differences in student achievement and perceived abilities. Teachers who emphasize effort rather than ability are more likely to motivate their students to do their best (Hunter & Barker, 1989). It is important, then, to communicate to your students that effort counts and that success is not measured by just a grade but also by improvement and progress.

Activity

6.2 Write an encouraging statement for each behavior below:

Student Behavior	Encouraging Remark
Maddie scores a 70% on her spelling test but is disappointed.	
Tom is stuck on a question and is becoming upset with himself.	
A group of students is having difficulty with a project and two members have decided to do it on their own.	

Interpersonal Relationships: Preventive and Supportive Strategies

Developing a climate that fosters relationships and respect can prevent many behavior problems. You should make eye contact with each of your students in the room, and move about. Don't stand behind a desk or podium-that signals a "stay away" attitude.
If a student offers an idea or an interesting question, attribute ownership to them. Say, *"Jim has an interesting question."*

It's often intriguing how adults will require youngsters to say "Please" and "Thank you" but forget to use those phrases themselves. By demonstrating courtesy, you are telling students you respect them. And don't get bent out of shape if your students don't return the courtesy at first. Be patient. They'll catch on.

> Be the model for the behavior you want in your students. That means, treat students with respect. Don't ridicule them, yell at them, call them names, or ignore them.

Another strategy to minimize behavior problems is to show an interest in your students by learning something about them and then communicating that to them. Greet your students at the door by their name and ask them about events or activities. Use their name in class when asking questions. Compliment students on their achievements outside of your class, *"Hey, Sondra, I saw you at the basketball game. Good job, there."* Send home positive notes or postcards or call home with a positive message, especially at the beginning of the year. If giving out gold stars or stickers is not your style, try pencils, bookmarks, or cookie coupons for the cafeteria. Everyone needs an "atta boy" so don't be shy about giving out compliments to your students.

Safe Environments

Safe environment refers not only to a student's physical safety but also to their emotional and mental safety. In Maslow's (1968) Need Hierarchy, safety is a deficiency need, deemed a lower-level need along with physiological, belongingness and esteem needs. If these needs are not fulfilled, Maslow hypothesized that higher needs, such as Knowing and Understanding, will not be met. If this premise is true, then students who feel threatened physically or mentally will not be inclined to learn.

How do you create a safe classroom? It means you will not tolerate bullying in your classroom. It means you and your students will not laugh at another student-for any reason. In a safe classroom, both teacher and students feel comfortable being themselves. It means it's OK to make mistakes in your class because we learn from our errors. How is this accomplished? Some teachers develop a tolerance-free classroom and teach about bullying, etc. Some teachers use interpersonal activities such as Get-to-Know-You activities. Others incorporate cooperative learning strategies on a regular basis. Still other teachers use variations on the class meeting.

Seating Arrangements

Research into classroom management also suggests that the room arrangement can be an effective prevention strategy. Marzano (2003) summarized that classroom arrangements should allow
1.   good visibility of all your students
2.   students to easily see all presentations and demonstrations
3.   for distribution and handling of materials
4.   good traffic flow (people can get around the room)
5.   for grouping of students into pairs, triads, and quads

Even though Dunn (2001) reports that the typical classroom arrangement of desks in neat rows makes it tough for teachers to freely walk around the classroom, this arrangement can be very flexible. For example, if there are six rows, students can be grouped into pairs using adjacent rows or teams of three or four.

Ramsden (1999) provides a good overview of the common seating arrangements with their positive and negative aspects. In her article she states,

Seating arrangements are very important when thinking about classroom management. The way a class should be arranged clearly depends on the type of students and the philosophies the teacher uses. In my view not one situation is better then [sic] *another and*

changing the room around will change the environment...Rows might be very successful for one student while clusters could be for another. All students learn differently and depending on the teacher's philosophy and the way the teacher incorporates the seating during the instruction has an influence on the students in different ways...A teacher needs to plan each seating arrangement carefully and look at all personalities and levels of students.

Your climate is influenced by the way your room looks. How would you feel in a room with bare walls, unpacked boxes stacked up against the wall, trash on the floor, and dirty, marred desks? You probably wouldn't want to touch anything let alone sit there for too long. Just how inviting is your classroom? Does it say to students *Come in. Spend some time here* or is it gloomy and unattractive? Does your room smell stuffy or have offensive odors? Creating your environment includes not only arranging the desks and tables but also cleaning and decorating the room. You can't do much about lighting and wall color, but you can make your room an attractive place to spend some time.

Activity

6.3 Design your ideal classroom

Activity

6.4 Sketch a bulletin board welcoming your students.

Recognizing Positive Behaviors

There are many informal ways to reward students for demonstrating appropriate behavior-both academic and social behaviors. An inexpensive way to recognize students is to display their work in the classroom. You can also read student essays to the class, their answers on tests, or responses to bellwork. Find ways to recognize students with statements such as, *John has a good question, Marcie makes a fine point, Lisa's concern has been the topic of much debate.* These informal methods go a long way to motivate students and minimize misbehaviors.

> We cannot hold a torch to light another's path without brightening our own. –Ben Sweetland.

Generate jobs for your students. Allow your students to help you with tasks such as passing out or collecting papers, cleaning the board, decorating the bulletin board, taking papers/messages to other teachers, or other tasks which can make students feel they are contributing to the class and are recognized by you. You might even consider roles that rotate throughout the year. These would include a classroom greeter who opens the door and "greets" people, a "teacher of the day" who helps with attendance, or a class librarian who might manage your classroom library.

There are other inexpensive ways to recognize students. You can use your computer to develop coupons that students can trade-in for prizes, pencils, paper or activities, such as free time, library time or computer time. If the entire class has earned a reward, you can arrange a day to play board games, a field day or a popcorn party. You might offer 10 minutes of listening to music, time for quiet talking with their friends, or opportunity for watching a video. A good way to find out what students like as rewards is to ask them. Be sure to check with your administration if the rewards are allowed in your school.

Activity

6.5 Think about a teacher who used positive methods of recognizing students and make a list that you might apply with your students.

Teaching Social Skills

Many children can benefit from learning social skills because they simply lack the social skills needed to work cooperatively with other children. Social skills can be taught just like academic skills. Social skills include: sharing, praising, using quiet voices, encouraging others, listening, and sharing ideas. To begin social skills instruction, first observe your students to determine what skill they might need. After you have made your list, select one skill to work on per week. According to Johnson, Johnson, and Holubec (1988), there are five steps in teaching social skills.

1. Discuss the need for the skill. Students should understand why the skill is important in and outside of the classroom.

2. Teach the skill. You have to show students exactly what the skill looks like and sounds like. A T-chart is an effective technique to use in this step. You can create a poster or a transparency. Write the social skill at the top and ask students to brainstorm what they do and say when they are demonstrating the social skill.

Praising	
Looks Like	Sounds Like

Examples of Looks Like: high five, thumbs up, smile
Examples of Sounds Like: *Good job! Yes! Good answer!*

3. Set up practice situations. If your goal is to teach praising, use a pair-share where one student answers a question and the other praises. Then have them reverse roles. If you want to teach the social skill of listening, then an appropriate practice activity is to use an interview technique. You will find many activities, or structures, in the work of Spencer Kagan (www.Kaganonline.com)

4. Reflect on the social skill. During the structured practice activity, use your quiet signal to stop the activity and ask students to think about how well they have been using the skill. If you have observed students doing a particularly good job, share your observations with the class.

5. Provide other activities for practice and encourage the use of the skill all week.

Even if you do not use cooperative learning groups, teaching social skills should be an essential part of your curriculum. The acquisition of social skills is vital for success in today's society and teaching these skills should be considered an indispensable component of your curriculum.

Activity

6.6 Develop a T-chart for a particular social skill that you will teach your students and brainstorm possible student answers to the Looks Like/Sounds Like columns.

Content and Climate: Corrective Strategies

Two strategies to use when correcting action needs to be taken are class meetings and conferences. These two approaches address the problem(s) as well as strengthen teacher-student relationships and help to maintain a positive climate in the classroom.

Class Meetings

A corrective strategy that gives students voice and encourages self-discipline is the use of class meetings. There is a considerable amount of literature on class meetings and you are encouraged to read and learn about the specifics of conducting them (Dreikurs, 1992; Styles, 2001, Wofgang, 2001)l. Here are some appropriate meeting topics:

➢ We're having a problem with tardies. How can we cut down on this?
➢ There's a lot of talking during bellwork and many of you are not completing it. What can we do to improve our entrance procedure?
➢ What are some ways to make new students feel comfortable?
➢ What is a good procedure so that everyone gets to use the computer?

Some teachers use the class meeting to allow students a voice in determining the rules of the classroom. It is advisable for you to begin the year with a set of rules to establish your desired climate. After you and your students have developed trust, then you can reexamine your class rules together in a meeting. Student involvement in rule making can be difficult particularly if you teach several classes, such as in middle and high school. In this case, each class should discuss rules that would be applicable for all your students. You should also hold the veto power over any rule you think is objectionable.

Meetings can also be effective in planning events. Students can be given a voice in how they want to celebrate a holiday, i.e. Veteran's Day, Thanksgiving, or in the selection of a field trip or guest speaker. You need to be aware that when you ask, *Where should we go on our next field trip?* you are leaving yourself open for suggestions such as Paris, Disney World, and Jamaica. Be prepared to either handle such suggestions with humor (*Not unless you pay my way.*) or as a teachable moment where students research the plausibility of such destinations.

Whether you use class meetings or not, try to find small opportunities to give students input into what's happening in their class.

Conferencing with Students and/or Parents

One of the essentials in teaching is ongoing communication between teacher and student and parent/home. Long before you have a formal conference with the student and parent, you should let all concerned know of potential concerns as they happen. The ways to accomplish this open communication are to send home periodic progress grade reports, include notes from you in the student's planner, send home scholarship warnings or make phone calls.

The Phone Conference

There's no easy way to tell a parent that their child is failing or not behaving in your class. Here are some guidelines for making that phone call home:

> One good teacher in a lifetime may sometimes change a delinquent into a solid citizen. –Philip Wylie

1. Have your documentation in front of you. You should have a complete record of the child's academic grades and missing assignments. In addition, you should have a log of the child's unusual or disruptive behavior.

2. Begin with an introduction. *Good morning, Mrs. Smith. This is Mr. Brown, Jason's math teacher.*

3. After the parent acknowledges you, tell them your concern and give a specific description of the behavior. *I'm calling because I'm concerned about Jason's progress. He's not turning in his homework. In fact, he has 5 homework assignments missing.*

4. Tell the parent what you've done so far. *I talked to Jason last week about this and he promised to make up the work. I also gave him a review sheet for the test. Unfortunately, he still hasn't turned in the work and he scored a failing grade on the test.*

5. You need to get information from the parent now so stop talking and wait for the parent to respond. If they don't respond, ask, *Is there something I should know that's preventing him from doing his homework?*

6. Because this conversation is more effective if brief, be ready to offer some ideas. Put forward some suggestions. *I'm going to make sure he's written down his homework assignments in his planner and initial it. If you'll ask to see it as well, maybe we can monitor Jason more closely.* If your suggestion doesn't meet with parental approval, ask, *What would you rather do?*

7. Now state your confidence in the plan. Tell the parent that you're going to work with the child on the plan. *I think this is a good plan. If we continue to work together, I'm sure Jason will get on track.*

8. Now you're almost done. Thank the parent for their cooperation. *Thank you so much Mrs. Smith for helping me with this. Let's keep in touch and feel free to call me.*

9. After you hang up the phone, write down the date and time of the call and what was decided. As soon as possible, tell the child what you talked about, how it was resolved, and if he's in agreement. *Hey, Jason. I just had a good talk with your mom about your missing homework and we talked about checking your planner every day. I'll initial it when you write the assignment and she'll check it when you get home. Does that sound reasonable to you?*

How early should you start making these phone calls home? These phone conferences should probably begin after the second week of school. The key is to keep parents informed. If the parent isn't home, leave a message that includes a good time to call you. What you don't want is for a parent to think all is well only to find at the end of the grading period that their child has failed your class.

Face-to-Face Conference

Inevitably, you may have to have that difficult face-to-face parent conference. Whether you or the parent requests it, the guidelines are similar to the phone call conference:

1. Be prepared. Bring all the relevant information, such as, grades, behavior logs, and communications home, ie, progress reports, scholarship warnings.
2. Get support from the guidance counselor or other teachers and invite them to the conference. Asking for help is not a sign of weakness.
3. Plan an agenda, time limit and possible solutions to the problem.

4.   Invite the student to the conference.

5.   Make sure you make special accommodations, such as an interpreter or translator, if the parent is deaf or does not speak English.

6.   Greet the parents and student warmly. Introduce everyone present. Briefly, make small talk to make them feel at ease.

7.   Begin the conference by stating the purpose. *I've called this conference because Shawn has not shown any progress this nine weeks in his academics or behavior.* State something positive about the child. *Shawn is a charming young man and has a creative streak that comes out in his writing.*

8.   Now give the facts. Bring out your documentation and let the parent look it over. Look at the child and say, *Shawn, what do you have to say?*

9.   Ask the parents for suggestions. Ask them what worked in the past or what they are willing to try.

10.   If the parent doesn't have a suggestion, offer one you already had in mind.

11.   Write down what you all agreed upon.

12.   When it's about five minutes away from the agreed upon time limit, say, *We only have five minutes left. Let's recap what we're each going to do.*

Even if you feel the conference did not accomplish anything, be sure to follow through on your part and continue to communicate with the parent. You need to always express your concern for the child and your willingness to help.

Activity

6.7 Develop a form requesting a parent conference. Be sure to list available times and days and a method of confirming the conference.

The three words that characterize effective classroom managers best are **prepared, flexible, and adaptable**. As you will see, making a plan is the foundation of classroom management. Most importantly, focusing on preventative and supportive strategies will reduce the possibility of behavior problems in your classroom.

We think of the effective teachers
we have had over the years with a
sense of recognition, but those who have
touched our humanity we remember
with a deep sense of gratitude. -Anonymous

Seven

Classroom Management: Communicating Expectations

Most behavior problems in the classroom can be prevented with good lesson planning, establishing a warm climate through interpersonal relationships, and giving students a voice in the classroom. It is estimated that the effective manager can prevent 80 to 90% of all behavior problems with careful planning. In addition, the creation of procedures to minimize lost allocated time, and the monitoring of student adherence to the classroom rules go a long way to keep the classroom functioning as a successful learning environment. That doesn't mean there won't be some problems. Let's examine strategies in establishing expectations for student behavior:

	Preventive Strategies	Supportive Strategies	Corrective Strategies
Expectation for Behavior	• Teaching & reteaching procedures • Creating and communicating rules and expectations	• Giving students voice • Providing recognition for positive behaviors • Conferencing with student and/or parent	• Using language of choice • Using assertive communication • Applying consequences fairly

.

Expectations for Behavior: Preventive and Supportive Strategies

Discipline is the topic most people think of as classroom management. Notice that in this model there are preventive and supportive strategies, and, when used, you might find you do not need to employ corrective strategies as often. Let's consider some of these.

Research by Marzano (2003) shows classrooms where rules and procedures were effectively implemented had fewer disruptions than in classes which did not, and this was true across all grade levels. However, just posting or telling students the rules is not enough. To be an effective strategy, rules and the reasons behind the rules must be explained and student input must be sought.

Rules

All places of business have rules of behavior. Your classroom is a place of work and, as such, needs to maintain order. One way is to establish your classroom rules. You need to consider how you want your students to behave in your classroom. Some general rules might include: *Respect others* or *Be polite*. These are OK but students may not know how respect and being polite translate into actual behavior. If you use this type of general rule, be sure to discuss and demonstrate what "polite" and "respect" mean. It's better to use more specific rules: *Listen to the speaker; Follow directions the first time they are given; Be on time; Stay seated unless you have permission to get up; Do not curse, call people names, or bully.*

Rules are the behaviors you expect your students to follow and, if they don't, there will be consequences. You should post the rules and consequences on the first day of school. Initially, you will want to refer to your rules when you correct a child's behavior. For example, Jane gets out of her seat without permission. Simply say, *Jane, the rule is to wait for permission to get up. Please be seated.* After the first few days, start enacting the consequences and continue to tell the student what rule was broken.

Experts believe that fewer rules are better than too many because they're easier to manage. Some teachers have one rule: *Respect individuals, their belongings and their ideas.* Other teachers have eight to ten rules. You must determine for yourself what rules you need for your classroom to operate in an orderly manner.

Teaching Rules

However many rules you develop, you need to present and teach each one (Canter, 2001; Freiberg, J. (1999). When you explain the rules, it is always wise to clarify the reason behind the rules even to young adults: *We can't eat or drink in class because it brings bugs and is a health hazard.* Have student discuss what the rule looks like, i.e. What does *"Keep your hands and feet to yourself"* look like in the classroom? Depending on the age of the student, you may want to role play examples and non-examples of the rule. Some teachers divide the class into groups after the discussion, and have them draw pictures of children following the rules. Older student can discuss the value of rules and what happens to a business or society without rules. What's important here is that you can't just post the rules. You must teach them also. There are many ways to teach rules as presented by Jones and Jones (2010), *Comprehensive Classroom Management.*

Rules should also match the climate you desire in your classroom (Borich,2006). In planning your rules, you should answer these questions: What rules do I need to

1. enhance the work setting and minimize disruptions?
2. promote the safety of all my students?
3. prevent disturbances to and between students?
4. promote courtesy and interpersonal relationships?

Class Rules
1. Listen to the speaker.
2. Stay seated unless given permission.
3. Keep your hands and feet to yourself.
4. Avoid loud talking or noises.
5. No horseplay, hitting, or fighting in the classroom.

Because you and your students have to live with the rules, try to avoid making a rule you cannot enforce consistently. You don't want to make a rule that applies only under certain conditions. For example, if you allow your students the freedom to get out of their seats to retrieve resource materials, then a rule which says, *Stay seated at all times*, cannot be applied all the time. Restated as, *Stay seated unless given permission or told otherwise,* provides the flexibility you might need. Your rules should allow for flexibility while providing the structure and limits needed to keep the work environment stable. It is also important to remember that if one of your rules isn't working, change it.

Consequences

So, if a student "breaks" a rule, what do you do? Remember that effective managers plan their consequences along with their rules (Canter, 2001). You will need to consider developing a hierarchy of consequences. After all, you can't send a student to the office on his/her first offense (unless it's for fighting). A sample list of formal consequences might look like this:

First - Warning
Second - Time out
Third - Call home
Fourth – Detention
Fifth – Lower Conduct Grade
Sixth- Referral

Ask other teachers at your school what are acceptable consequences and what works for them. You don't want to institute a consequence that is illegal or deemed inappropriate for the age level of the child. Once your rules and consequences have been established, make sure everyone, including parents, has a copy.

Management includes not only the planning of rules and consequences, but vigilance in implementing them. If a student breaks a rule, you cannot ignore it. You must deliver some type of consequence immediately, all the while keeping your instructional momentum. There are some non-intrusive methods and communication devices to get students back on track that you need to add to your toolbox.

Non-intrusive management

You can stop most misbehavior in the classroom with informal, non-intrusive techniques before you impose a formal consequence. Here are some examples (Albert,1989):

1. Proximity control – the teacher moves next to or near the student(s) who are not on task. Simply being close-by may alert the student to refocus on the task.

2. Deflecting – the teacher reminds the student(s) by reminding the class what they are supposed to be doing, i.e. *We're all supposed to be writing an introduction.*

3. Non-verbal signal – the teacher uses a non-verbal signal to alert the student(s) they are off-task, such as a finger to mouth, quiet hand, or hand signal for "NO." The teacher does not interrupt the lesson but, rather, makes eye contact and then signals to the student(s).

4. Proximal praise – the teacher praises a student near the student misbehaving for the behavior desired, i.e. misbehaving-Todd is sitting near Wesley. *Wesley, you're working very hard on your project. You should complete it on time.* Todd hears the praise and refocuses.

> Praise publicly, discipline privately.

5. Hand on student's desk- the teacher walks over to the student, continues with the lesson and waits for the student to get back on track (proximity). After 10-15 seconds, if the student does not refocus, the teacher places his/her hand on the student's desk and taps quietly.

6. Ask student a question – the teacher poses a question and asks the inattentive or misbehaving student. This can be tricky because you don't want to make the student feel unintelligent. If they don't know the answer, say, *Think about it. I'll come back to you.* (Be sure to "get back to them") Please note the teacher does not say, *If you were listening, you'd know the answer.* We don't want to embarrass them, just refocus them.

Activity

7.1 Develop a set of 5-8 rules for your classroom. Then write your consequences. When complete, write a letter to parents explaining your system of behavioral management.

Record Keeping

You need to devise a method that will allow you to keep a record of rule infractions and also not disturb the learning climate. For example, keep a clipboard with a roster of student names near you. If a student misbehaves, employ one of the nonintrusive methods. If the student does not respond appropriately, simply say the student's name, the rule broken, what the student should do, and mark down on your roster the rule number next to the student's name. It might go like this: Lucas gets out of his seat to go to the pencil sharpener. You make eye contact and give a hand signal to return to his seat. He does not, but continues toward the sharpener. You say, *Lucas, you got out of your seat without permission. Please sit down. Thank you* and mark your roster. When you can, call Lucas to your desk or ask him to see you after class. Privately discuss your concerns and listen to what Lucas has to say.

Some teachers like to use public recording methods, such as names on the board or on a transparency. These methods can backfire if the student is misbehaving because he/she is looking for attention. By writing their name on the board and putting checks by their name, you have just given them the attention they sought. Record keeping should always be private.

Another effective and quiet method of instituting private consequences is to use color-coded index cards or post-it notes. Say a student is talking and disturbing those around him who are trying to complete seatwork. You walk over (proximity), praise those near him for being on task (proximal praise), but the student continues being off-task. Now you place a yellow card on the student's desk. If the student says, *What's this for?* Say, *You are talking and disturbing others around you. This is a warning.* If the student continues, you place a red card on his/her desk and say, *You have earned a Time Out. Please follow me.* Don't forget to keep a record of the infraction.

If, after the yellow card is given, the student shapes up and does not misbehave again, be sure to praise him/her for making a good choice and express your appreciation. The color-coded cards are particularly effective during group work.

Activity

7.2 Research different methods of recording behavior and describe the method you will use. Be as specific as you can in your description.

Rewards

It's important to balance negative consequences with positive rewards. The simplest and cheapest positive consequences are specific praise, smiles, thumbs up, or any signal that says you appreciate your students' behavior. When praising, be sure to use specific praise, that is, tell them what behavior was noticed: *Thank you, class, for continuing to work quietly during that interruption* or *During group work, you stayed focused, didn't raise your noise level, and everyone completed their work. Great job!*

Here are some guidelines for effective praise (Kizlik, 2005):
- It is delivered contingently upon student performance of desirable behaviors or real accomplishment
- Praise specifies the excellent aspects of the student's accomplishment.
- It is expressed sincerely.
- Praise is offered for genuine effort, progress or accomplishments judged according to a criterion.
- It helps the student appreciate their own thinking processes.
- It attributes student success to effort and ability rather than ability alone.

Other rewards may include recognition by the following techniques: displaying student work, phone calls home with good news, student photographs on bulletin board, or *student of the week* (or month) awards. You can also give students privileges like helping the teacher with passing out materials, taking attendance, being a peer tutor, and grading papers. Computer time, library passes, and "free" time certificates are other inexpensive ways to positively reward students.

> The kids in our classroom are infinitely more significant than the subject matter we teach.
> – Meladee McCarty

Alderman (1997) advises to use caution with free time rewards in the classroom especially during the first few months of school. If free time rewards are given, he suggests they be celebrated outside the classroom. In this manner, students associate the classroom with learning and you establish a clear expectation for behavior in the classroom that focuses on the lesson being taught, not on "fun" activities.

You might want to institute a regular system of rewards by sending home Positive Postcards. This can be costly but sometimes there's money available through mini grants or other school funds to pay for postage and postcards. Certificates can be awarded weekly, monthly, or for the grading period for various achievements in the academic as well as the behavioral area.

Some students do not like public acknowledgment; therefore, positive statements on their papers, post-it notes with specific praise, or stamps and stickers will do the trick. You can use the *See Me After Class* technique where you talk individually with the student without his/her peers present. Whenever possible, you should use positive methods to support and reinforce the behavior you want in your classroom.

Activity

7.3 List the positive rewards you will use with your students. You might divide these into academic and behavioral rewards.

Procedures

Ms. Martino has stopped the information-sharing portion of the class and says, *I need your homework before you leave.* All at once, ten of her students rise from their seats to hand in their assignments. While she is busy collecting and stacking the papers, several boys in the back of the room start poking each other and three girls begin walking toward the door. The bell rings and Ms. Martino yells, *Don't forget your homework assignment. It was written on the board. Have a good day!*

In this scenario, Ms. Martino does not appear to have procedures for passing in papers or for exiting the class. Wong (2002) states that the major problem in most classrooms is not discipline but the lack of procedures. Think about it: If there wasn't a checkout procedure at the grocery store, there would be chaos during busy shopping hours. Without procedures for boarding an airplane, well… you get the drift. Your classroom is no different.

Procedures are how you want things done in your classroom. Effective managers teach their procedures during the first weeks of school and reinforce them the entire year. One distinction between rules and procedures is that negative consequences are not given if a student does not follow a procedure. We simply remind the student of the procedure and reteach it if necessary.

You will need to determine the procedures you need so your classroom will run smoothly. Some procedures to consider are: entering a room, exiting the room, heading papers, sharpening pencils, turning in papers, getting work after an absence, and keeping a notebook. Some "rules" such as *Have your pencil sharpened before class begins* are actually procedures. Do you really want to refer a student for not sharpening his/her pencil at the right time?

Teaching Procedures

Teach your procedures just like you teach your rules.

Heading Your Paper
• 1st line-Full Name • 2nd line-Class & Period • 3rd line-Date • 4th line-Assignment

1. Post the procedures, especially at the beginning of the year.
2. Explain the procedure and demonstrate it.
3. Practice the procedure. If you're explaining *Heading Your Paper*, provide a model and practice the procedure every time there is an assignment requiring students to head their paper.
4. Reinforce with cues until it becomes a habit. Remind students to *Head your paper correctly* until students do so without prompting.

Activity

7.4 For each of the events that follow, write your procedure. There's room to add a procedure for your specific situation.

Entering the Classroom	
Quieting the Class	
Turning in Assignments	
Passing out/in papers	
Dismissing the Class	

Finishing work early	

Clearly, preparing a management plan that includes the rules, consequences and procedures will prevent many behavioral problems from ever happening. And while rules and consequences should be applied consistently, effective managers allow for flexibility. This does not mean that you will give consequences to some students and not others for breaking the same rule. It means that you might need to be flexible in <u>when</u> you apply the rule. For example, your rule states, *Raise your hand for permission to speak,* however, during group work, you allow students to speak without getting "permission" from you. While you might be tempted to get rid of your speaking rule, it is more desirable to clearly delineate when the rule is and is not in effect.

Good managers are adaptable. If your rules and procedures are not working, change them. Tell students, *We have a problem.* Albert Einstein once defined *insanity* as: doing the same thing over and over again and expecting different results. If your classroom management plan does not produce the results you want in student behavior, do something different.

Giving Students Voice

For the most part, teachers make all the decisions in the classroom: what to read, what to write about, how many math problems to solve, where to sit, when the assignment is due, etc. One method of preventing misbehavior is to give students voice. Providing students a voice means allowing them, within guidelines, to make small decisions. Here are some examples:

- *Do you want to do the odd or even problems today?*
- *Would you like to read the assignment on your own or with a buddy?*
- *Which date do you prefer for your due date: Wednesday or Thursday?*
- *Choose one of these topics to write about. If you have another topic, check with me first.*
- *You can pick one of these methods to show your research: pamphlet, oral presentation, written report or poster or What are some ways you can share your research with the class? Let's list them.*
- *How much time do you need for this task, 15 or 20 minutes?*

Notice that the choices have structure. The choice is not *What do you want to study?* but, rather, students choose from a well thought-out list. Obviously, you will not be able to allow student choice in every situation. But finding ways to give students power in the classroom is a healthy way to teach self-discipline and reduce misbehaviors. There's another benefit. Imagine the class decided on a due date for their project and a student didn't turn it in. Instead of the student (or parent) accusing you of an unreasonable timeline, you can simply say, *The class decided on the date. Why didn't you speak up if it was a problem?*

When you allow student voice in your classroom, you eliminate the idea that students are "empty vessels" for teachers to fill with knowledge. The KWL strategy is an excellent active learning device, focused on content and that can be used to give students' voice.

What I Know	What I Want to Know	What I Learned

At the start of a unit or topic, the teacher leads the class, small groups, or individuals in completing the first two columns of the chart using an overhead or on large chart paper. As students work through the unit, refer to the "What I Want to Know" column to see if their questions have been answered. At the end of the unit, a class discussion on "What I Learned" can serve as a review. Any unanswered questions can be addressed or students might volunteer to search for the answers. The important thing to consider is that in using KWL, students provide teachers with information at the beginning of a unit that can help shape the course of study and increase student motivation in the topic.

Expectations for Behavior: Corrective Strategies

Activity

7.5 Did you ever misbehave in school? If not, how about your friends? Think back and list the possible reason(s) for the misbehavior. What could the teacher or school have done to prevent such behaviors?

Possible Causes of Student Misbehavior

Even though you have prepared and planned, you may encounter a student who just won't follow the rules and procedures of your classroom. By the way, there's a big difference between one child, a group of students, and the majority of students misbehaving. The difference is the scale of the problem. While one child's behavior may be serious enough to disrupt your classroom, when the majority of the students misbehave, you either don't have a management plan or the plan in place isn't working. Whichever the case, you need to examine the cause(s) of the problem.

If there are groups of students or the majority of your class is off-task or engaging in minor disruptions, you need to ask yourself these questions: Do I have engaging lessons with active learning components? Have I established a warm and inviting climate? Did I teach my rules effectively and do I vigorously monitor those rules? Do I have procedures in place and did I teach and reinforce those procedures?

If you can honestly answer "yes" to all those questions and you still have disruptions, then you need to examine why the students are misbehaving. There are many theories as to why individuals misbehave. Some believe it is because of an unanswered need, such as attention, power or revenge. Others consider the student's need for confidence or love. Still others examine the avoidance of failure or frustration. Whatever approach you ascribe to, you will agree that students misbehave for a reason. Let's consider some of those motives (Albert, 1989; Glasser,1986; Munk, 1994; Myers-Walls, 2004)

<u>Health and Stressors</u>

When you don't get enough sleep, food, exercise, or relaxation time, do you get cranky? So do children. Under these circumstances, they are often irritable, fussy or grouchy. The best strategy is simply to ask the child if he/she is feeling OK. Just showing concern may be the best way to disarm a child. If a child is ill, refer him/her to the nurse or have them call their parent/guardian.

Stressors in the child's life can cause a behavior change. If there was a death in the family, separation or divorce, parental unemployment, or serious illness of a loved one, the child may react inappropriately to the slightest prompt. In these situations, it's best to refer the student to the school counselor or other professional and always be empathic with the student. The father of a sixth grade student died unexpectedly and upon his return to school, his teacher gave him a "Need to Leave Class" pass so he could see the counselor immediately if needed. Interestingly, he said he really appreciated being given the pass even though he never used it. Be careful, though. In real life, adults do not dodge their responsibilities because of personal issues. Students can be given some "slack" but it can be risky in the long run to let them "off the hook."

<u>Lack of Knowledge and Experience</u>

Sometimes children really don't know any better. Children are not adults and do not think like adults. When you ask, *What were you thinking?* they may not have been thinking but, in fact, reacting. It is our job to help children develop thinking skills and create in them an awareness of others. In these situations, it's best to ask, *When you _____ what happens to _____?* (Example: When you call people names, how do they feel?) This approach can help the student to think outside himself/herself.

Another area in which students may lack knowledge is social skills. They lack some of the basic skills for interacting with their classmates simply because no one taught them. If they do not know how to share or take turns, then it's our job to teach them. (See the T-Chart in Ch. 5)

Discouraged or Lack of Confidence

Children who have experienced failure or who do not feel good about themselves as students, may act out to avoid academic tasks or may take a passive approach and refuse to work. Children need a "can do" attitude in school and it's your job to give it to them.

Besides giving encouraging statements and specific praise, you can help students through careful monitoring, praising their effort, holding short one-on-one conferences, and making statements, such as, *What do you need to get started?* or *I know this is hard to understand, but we're going to take it slow.* or *Let's start at the beginning and take it one step at a time.*

A student's request for help can take many forms. Sometimes they will say they don't understand. On other occasions, they may simply refuse to do the work. These students are afraid to try and fail again. While it may be frustrating for you, do not ignore their calls for help.

> Ignoring can be dangerous. Sometimes, ignoring says to the child that you allow it. If you allow it, you teach it.

Habit

In some cases, students have been rewarded for their misbehaviors. A parent might encourage and reinforce behaviors such as "sticking up for yourself" by fighting and hitting. Adults giving in to tantrums may reinforce this behavior. Parents or adults who allow a child to interrupt their conversations, may raise students who interrupt your lesson. Sometimes, ignoring misbehaviors is a method of reinforcing the very behavior you do not want.

If a child steals and the parent and/or teacher ignores it, the child may think it's OK to steal. Children who break toys, destroy their friend's or sibling's belongings, or deface or ruin school property without consequence, are being reinforced for their behavior. Over time, if undesirable behaviors are ignored or inconsistently corrected, the child may engage in these behaviors without even being conscious of them. Depending on the age of the child, habitual misbehavior can be difficult to change, and you will need to teach new, acceptable behaviors to replace the unacceptable ones.

Anger or Power

Sometimes kids get angry. Maybe another student or adult embarrassed them in public or chastised them for something minor. Maybe someone stole their cell phone or their parent won't let them go home with a friend. Feeling angry can manifest itself in acting out at people that weren't responsible for the hurt feelings to begin with. Developing a caring relationship with the child and fostering a caring environment in your classroom will go a long way to prevent angry confrontations.

Then there are the children who need to be in control of your classroom. They seem to scream, *I want to do it my way or not at all!* These individuals may talk back, be defiant, disrespectful, or throw a tantrum. A passive individual will appear to agree and then sit back and not do what you requested or do it his or her own way. Giving students voice can help meet their need for power and control, and there are some communication techniques that you can acquire that will go a long way to avoid confrontations.

Should angry confrontations start brewing, don't ignore the rumblings. While you may want to fire back a retort at a student who called you "dumb," bite your tongue. Your angry response will only escalate the student's reaction. Instead, remain composed and table the discussion by saying, *Let's talk about this later.* If the student refuses to work, acknowledge his/her power by calmly saying, *I can't make you do your work. However, you cannot prevent others from doing theirs by disturbing them.*

Boredom

"Boring is the opposite of fun." (Glasser,1986). Face it, when we enjoy ourselves, time goes by quickly and we hate it when we have to stop the activity. But if we're bored, we can't wait to escape, and children will find ways to make a boring activity more interesting or to end the pain of a monotonous lesson. They will sigh loudly, begin talking to their neighbors, draw, read magazines, or engage in otherwise unacceptable behaviors.

> No use to shout at them to pay attention. If the situations, the materials, the problems before the child do not interest him, his attention will slip off to what does interest him, and no amount of exhortation or threats will bring it back. – John Holt

Planning interesting lessons with active learning strategies and connecting the learning to students' previous knowledge and interests is the best preventative. It is also important to recognize that not all learning is fun and acknowledging that to your students may ease some of these behaviors. *Ok, this part of the chapter may not be exciting to you but we have to cover it. Let's pay attention so we can get to the most interesting section.*

Attention

We all need to feel that someone knows we exist. When we feel ignored or need personal contact with others, we seek it out. Children may not know the appropriate ways to seek attention so they may disrupt the class, annoy you, or annoy their classmates. *Teacher, Jose is bothering me!* Children with a more passive approach may appear to be slow to act. Everyone has their book out except Kiana who's waiting for you to tell her personally to get out her book. (And when you do that, you have just reinforced that behavior.)

If you provide positive recognition for appropriate behaviors in your classroom, some attention-seeking behaviors will diminish. Many non-intrusive techniques can also work with students seeking attention, such as proximity, making eye contact, and sending a nonverbal signal. If the behaviors continue, you may need to hold a conference with the student and discuss appropriate ways to gain your attention. In extreme cases, you may need to change the student's seat or use time out and remove him/her from the activity for a short time.

Handling Misbehavior Through Communication

Assertive Communication

It is essential that you use respectful language, both verbal and body, in talking with your students. Generally, that means that you talk relatively quietly, avoid sarcasm, use self-control, discuss the behavior and not the child, and that your facial expressions and body language are assertive, not hostile. (Alderman, 1997).

> Address it and drop it. – Terry Alderman

Assertive communication is a method you can use to express what behaviors you want to stop and what behaviors you want the student to start. Along with the words you say, your body language must also say, *This is what I want.* Make eye contact with the student, keep your body erect, keep your facial expression calm and speak clearly but without yelling. Then state: (Name) *please stop* (behavior) *and begin* (behavior). It would sound like this:

- ❖ *Jared, please stop talking and begin your seatwork.*
- ❖ *Monica, stop playing with your purse and get started on your math.*
- ❖ *Ignacio, get focused on your reading and stop staring out the window.*

Another strategy is the I message. In this type of assertive communication the format is: *When you* (statement of the problem), *then* (effect), *and I feel* (emotion). For example,

- ❖ *Jennie, when you talk out like that, it interrupts the lesson and I feel frustrated. Please listen and wait to be recognized.*
- ❖ *Class, when you fill the aisles with your stuff, I cannot walk safely around to help you and that distresses me.*
- ❖ *Erinesia, I feel uncertain as to how to help you when you won't even try to write a sentence because I don't know what you need.*

Also effective is the lawyer strategy. After you have given an assertive statement and the behavior continues, try using the "yes or no" technique. Here's how it sounds:

- ❖ *Tina and Maria, please stop talking and begin your work.*

They nod at you and then continue to talk.

- ❖ *Tina and Maria, I asked you to stop you conversation and start your work. Are you going to begin, yes or no?*

7.6 Write an assertive response to each situation below.

Student Behavior	Your Response
During your lesson presentation, Tina gets out of her seat and starts sharpening her pencil.	
Luis and Steven are talking and laughing during your lesson. Children near them are distracted.	
After you gave directions for seatwork, Marlena put her head on her desk.	
Small groups are working quietly. Suddenly Anthony tears up the group's project and says, *This is dumb!*	

Language of Choice

An assertive communication method designed to get students to think about their actions is to use the language of choice. Here, you provide students with a choice regarding their behavior.

- ❖ *You may clean your work station now or I'll arrange with your next teacher for you to stay after class to clean up. It's your choice.*
- ❖ *Which do you prefer-working with your group or doing the whole assignment alone?*
- ❖ *You can choose to focus on your assignment or, if you continue to disrupt, go to time out.*

Using language of choice gives students legitimate power. You hope, of course, that they will make the appropriate choice. If they do, acknowledge it. *You've made a good choice.* If they refuse to make a choice, indicate you must make the choice for them. *I'm sorry you refuse to make a good choice. You will need to take your work to Mr. Harris' room.*

A caution is in order here. If you want the student to focus on the assignment, then don't give choices students will select that are not academically related. For example, *You may choose to work on your math or play on the computer. Which would you choose?* Rephrase the choice in the following manner: *You may choose to work on your math here or go to Mr. Holt's room to do your work.* (Make sure you've arranged with Mr. Holt for this type of time out.)

7.7 Write a statement with each situation below that uses language of choice:

Student Behavior	Language of Choice
Chris does not turn in a project that was assigned two weeks ago. He comes to your desk and asks for extra credit work.	
Chareese is not working with her group and has moved away from the table.	
In the middle of your lesson Jordan is drawing pictures unrelated to the content. When you stand near him, he looks up and says, *We had this last year and it's still boring.*	
Katie never has paper, pencil or pen. You gave a supply list and even loaned her paper and pencil. It is the start of the 3rd week of school and she still does not have supplies.	

Stages of Intervention

Even though you've followed through with all the preventive strategies, sometimes you will have to react with corrective ones. Unless the safety of the child or other children is in question, it's best to proceed in stages rather than to jump to a severe consequence.

Here's how it works:

Strategy	Situation: Tammy is not working on her seatwork assignment and is quietly humming.
1. Nonverbal Cues Begin by making eye contact with the student and a signal (shake head, finger to lip, etc.)	Teacher makes eye contact, shakes head no-no and points to paper.
2. Use Proximity Walk over to the student and stand nearby .	Teacher stands near Tammy.
3. Redirect the behavior Quietly tap on the student's desk, or redirect the behavior by saying, *You should be working on the comprehension questions.*	*Tammy, what do you need to get started? Nothing? Great. Let's try the first problem.* Teacher walks away and Tammy reverts to old behavior.

4. Give a brief verbal desist
    Quietly deliver an assertive
    communication.
	Tammy, when you hum and play with your hair, you can't get your work done and then I am disappointed. You may choose to continue this behavior or sit in the think chair for the remainder of the period.

5. Deliver a moderate consequence
    Moderate consequences include removal to
    classroom time-out, or a seating change.
	Tammy puts her head down.
	Tammy, your behavior says you've chosen the Think Chair.

6. If the behavior continues, you should deliver a more intensive consequence, such as sending the student to another location for time out.	Tammy moves to the time-out Think Chair and begins to sing loudly. Teacher says: *Tammy, now you've chosen to disturb the entire class with your singing and noises. This is unacceptable. You must go to Mrs. King's class.* If child refuses to move the teacher says, *Your behavior is forcing me to call administration and have you removed from our class.* If child still refuses, the teacher calls administration and asks for assistance.

This type of intervention provides the least amount of interruption to your lesson and the quiet desists in stages 3, 4, and 5 will preserve order without negatively affecting the classroom climate.

With the advent of cell phones, some teachers like to call the parent at stage 5. This practice puts forth serious concerns over privacy and confidentially, as other students will, no doubt, hear the conversation with the parent. If the teacher and student leave the room for the call, then the remaining students are not supervised and this could be considered negligence. The safest approach is to call the student's parent/guardian during your conference time or after school.

> If you're on your cell phone, then you're not teaching or monitoring your students.

Activity

7.8 Decide on your first approach with each situation and a second if your first did not produce the desired behavior.

Situation	First Approach	Second Approach
Sierra and Mercy are talking constantly during the lesson presentation.		

Situation	First Approach	Second Approach
Mike bumped into Jessie accidentally outside. In the classroom, Mike makes a derogatory remark about Jessie loud enough for all to hear. Jessie stands up with raised fists.		
In the middle of your activity, Deidra yells out, *I don't understand this. It's the only class I'm confused in.*		

As a teacher, your focus should always be on teaching appropriate behaviors. Try to provide warmth and encouragement after correcting a student's behavior because the very children who act out are the ones who need our acceptance and support.

Developing and Refining Your Skills

No matter how perfect your management plan, no matter how terrific your lessons, there will be times when children act out. You might present a lesson that was successful four times and on the fifth try, it was a disaster. Your management plan may work with 99% of your students but there's one percent for whom you need special help. What to do?

We can always learn new ideas from your colleagues so don't be afraid to ask for help. If you're having difficulty with a student, it is possible other teachers are having the same problems and are willing to work on a solution. You might consider enrolling in a workshop or college course on management. An excellent web site that can provide you with concrete steps to deal with a specific behavior problem is: http://www.disciplinehelp.com.

As a professional educator, you should develop a desire to continuously expand your knowledge about teaching and children. To that end, work with your mentors and peers to create learning communities designed to increase your skills as a teacher. The professional

> You can observe a lot by just looking around. –Yogi Berra

literature on effective teaching including management of student behavior is vast and continuously growing. Your school library should have professional journals. If not, you and each of your colleagues might consider subscribing to at least one journal, or one journal each, and sharing it amongst yourselves.

Lastly, watch good teachers. Observe and listen to them as they work with children. Constantly learning and growing as a teacher will help you be successful and fulfilled in your profession.

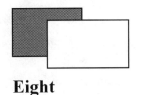

Eight

Teaching reading IS rocket
science. -Louisa Moats

Enhancing Students' Reading Comprehension

You are probably aware that reading is a complex process and one that continuously develops throughout our lives. Yet, teachers are dismayed on a daily basis when their students read material earmarked for their curriculum and they come away with little or no comprehension of what they read. To add to a teacher's frustration, high-stakes standardized testing measuring reading comprehension hangs like a cloud over every teacher's head. Consider: if the students cannot read and comprehend classroom material, how will they perform on a standardized test or in the real world?

We should all be concerned with our students' comprehension skills and it is, indeed, our responsibility to develop those skills. We will not explore here how to teach beginning reading or how to work with struggling readers. Rather, we will examine the dimensions that facilitate and enhance comprehension and should be a part of every classroom.

The extensive research over the years indicates there are at least five features, which, if instituted in your classroom, will help your students comprehend and learn. (Fielding & Pearson, 1994, Allington, 2002, and Rose, 2001). These features are:
1. giving background and connecting to students' prior knowledge;
2. providing a strong vocabulary program;
3. setting aside ample opportunity for actual reading and writing in the classroom;
4. allowing time for students to talk about the reading; and
5. incorporating teacher directed instruction and modeling of reading/thinking strategies.

Whether you're teaching kindergarten or high school, these five features are essential components to include in your classroom.

Connecting to Prior Knowledge

Prior knowledge is defined as all of an individual's previous learning and experiences. Research tells us that learning is enhanced when new information is integrated with the learner's existing knowledge (Rumelhart, 1980, Adams & Bertram, 1980). This is not a new concept in education, and, in fact, the connection between an individual's prior knowledge and reading comprehension has been clearly demonstrated over time (Christen, W. L. & Murphy, T. J., 1991).

There are two kinds of prior knowledge that are significant for you to consider; one is text-specific knowledge and the second is topic-specific knowledge. (Cooper, 2003). Text-specific knowledge refers to how the writing is organized. For example, narrative text tells a story usually organized in a sequential pattern and includes certain story elements such as plot, characters, setting, etc. Expository text is organized to communicate factual

> **T**here is an art of reading, as well as an art of thinking, and an art of writing.
> - Isaac Disraeli

information using patterns such as cause-and-effect, comparison-contrast, time-orientation (as with a sequence of events), main idea-details, description, or a combination of these patterns. Knowledge of text structure is important in the construction of passage meaning.

Topic-specific knowledge is knowledge about the information to be read or studied and includes key concepts and vocabulary. Background information on expository text usually correlates to the topic. With narrative, or story, text, prior knowledge is determined by the story line. For example, if students will be reading a novel about survival during a tsunami, they might profit from information about tsunamis, especially if they've never experienced one. If the students are going to read historical fiction, they may benefit from background on the time period.

Providing background knowledge can be direct, such as a field trip, experiment, or examination of an object; or indirect when students view a video, watch a demonstration, read a passage, or participate in a discussion. Good readers draw on their prior knowledge and experience to increase understanding, so when you teach students how to connect to the text, you are giving them a tool to better understand what they are reading (Christen & Murphy, 1991).

You can activate the students' prior knowledge by preteaching vocabulary, providing experiences relevant to the learning, or presenting the background information or concepts related to the topic. There are several simple methods that both uncover just how much students already know about a topic and can also activate their prior knowledge.

1. Prepared questions: What's an earthquake? What happens during an earthquake? Where do they usually occur? Why do they occur?
2. Word connection: When you hear the words *infection, pathogen, bacteria and virus,* what do you think of?
3. Call to mind: Tell me what you know about _____.
4. Group Brainstorming

    In group brainstorming, students in groups of 3-4 and are given one piece of paper and one pencil/pen. You ask the question: What do you know about _____? In turn, students orally say one thing they know, write it down on the paper, and pass the paper and pen to the member on their left. This continues until members do not have anything else to contribute or time is called. Their responses are then shared with the class.

5. KWL (Ogle, 1986)

    The KWL is a classic strategy where students brainstorm what they know (K) about a topic, generate questions they have (W), and finally, at the end of the learning experience, record what they learned (L). This strategy can be completed individually, in small groups or as a whole class activity. Young children can complete this activity if you write their responses using an overhead or chart paper.

What I Know	What I Want to Learn	What I Learned

6. ABC Brainstorming (Santa, Havens, & Valdes., 2004)
In this technique, students write the alphabet down the side of a sheet of notebook paper. Working individually or with a partner, students brainstorm terms associated with the topic that begin with each letter of the alphabet. If you're working with young children, you can have chart paper with the alphabet letters and let the group brainstorm while you write their responses.

7. Think-Aloud (Davey, 1983)
In this procedure, you read aloud and talk through your thought processes, in essence, modeling for students how to connect your prior knowledge to the text. For example, you might use key phrases such as: *This reminds me of..., This makes me think of..., This is similar to ...*

You can also describe your mental images, like: *When I read this title, in my mind I see... When I think of fractions, I see a pizza divided into eight pieces...*

When you read the title, say, *I know about _____. I saw a program on TV about this. It showed how...*

8. Preview and Predict

There are a variety of ways to preview what students will read or view. One method that focuses on background knowledge is PReP (Langer, 1981). The first phase of this technique is to engage students in a group discussion around the key ideas or concepts. You can begin the discussion with phrases, such as, *What do you think about when you hear...? What do you think of ...? What might you see, hear or feel when...?* Following the free association, you can encourage students to explain their responses.

Another preview method is to ask students to look over the material. If it's a textbook, you can ask students to skim the chapter title, headings and subheadings, and read the summary paragraph. If it's a narrative story book, have students scan the title, and "read" the pictures. If it's a novel, or chapter book, direct students to read the title, back cover and predict the setting and characters. After surveying, you can ask students to predict what they think the reading will be about, what type of material it is, what words they might encounter, or what questions the reading might answer.

9.   Preteach Vocabulary with semantic mapping
Semantic mapping is a spider web-like diagram
with the topic written in the center and related
concepts written on rays drawn out from the
center. Write the major concept in the center and
draw a circle around it. Then have students
brainstorm as many words or phrases that are
related to the topic. Write them on rays drawn out
from the center circle. Then guide the students to
group the words or ideas. As there is no one way
to complete a semantic map, application is only
limited by your imagination.

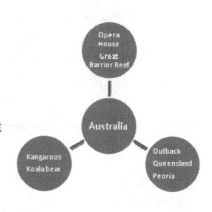

10.   Reading Aloud to students (Cooper, 2003)
In this strategy, you would select material that is related to the topic or story, tell
students why you are reading it to them, and give them a purpose for listening (*As I
read, I want to you listen for the characteristics of a tsunami.*) Read the selection
aloud and follow it with a discussion. Be sure you check if students grasped the
purpose of the reading.

11.   Direct and Indirect experiences
Using concrete materials and real experiences are critical in developing prior
knowledge. Students might look at microscope slides of human blood to examine
blood cells, examine different leaves, listen to different pieces of music or measure
different objects using various measurement devices. But if you cannot provide
these experiences, pictures, videos, or using the Internet can give similar
information. Be sure to tell your students how the experience is related to the topic
or story they will be reading.

Activity

8.1 Locate a curriculum guide for the grade/subject you will teach and select a unit.
Develop a strategy for developing students' prior knowledge and/or a method of
connecting to their background knowledge for this unit/topic.

Strong Vocabulary Program

Children are sometimes able to pronounce words
without knowing their meaning. Vocabulary is not the
act of correct pronunciation but, rather, the possession
of a broad base of word meanings, which is a basic
component of comprehension. Words consist of both

> Helping children build vivid and
> vital vocabularies is a crucial goal in
> helping all children become the very
> best readers and writers they can be.
> – P. M. Cunningham & R. L.
> Allington

general vocabulary, which are not associated with any one subject area, and technical
vocabulary which are uniquely related to a specific academic area. Students do not
automatically learn word meanings because they are exposed to them. To increase

118

comprehension and learning, you need to institute a strong vocabulary acquisition program where new words are directly taught and reinforced.

To begin, you will need to identify those words that may present difficulty for your students.   Choose words that:
- Are key concepts
- Have multiple meanings
- Are indispensable to understanding the reading

Probably the least effective strategy to teach vocabulary is to present a list of words, have students look up their definitions, write a sentence with each word, and then give a test at the end of the week. In order to truly learn new words, students must be immersed in words in meaningful ways and through repeated exposure to those words. (Stahl, 1986, Reutzel & Cooter, 2005) Teaching students to be aware of words and their importance to understanding is key to an effective vocabulary program.

Vocabulary Development Strategies

1. Word collection methods

   a. Word Walls (Cunningham,2007; Tompkins,1998; Wagstaff, 1999)
   A word wall is an organized collection of words that are displayed on a section of wall or on large chart paper designated for recording vocabulary words. Word walls are designed to promote learning, serve as permanent records of language learning, and can be easily integrated into daily literacy activities. There are many types of word walls you can develop, such as "Words We Know," and "ABC Wall." You might create a unit word wall. As you study a unit or story, you and your students write interesting, confusing, or important words from stories, informational books, and textbooks. One value of the word wall is that students can refer to the words in writing activities. Once a unit is completed, students can transfer the words onto index cards or a notebook.

   b. Word Banks or Notebooks
   Vocabulary notebooks can be effective if they focus on getting meaning from context. There are many ways students can enter words into their notebooks so you shouldn't be limited to a word-definition method. Below and to the right are examples of an entry method using context for word meaning.

   > Homeostasis
   > 1. The body's return to normal after a scare is one example of <u>homeostasis</u>.
   > 2. def.: staying normal
   > 3. My def.: process keeping internal temperature stable
   > 4. It's important for warm-blooded animals to maintain homeostasis.

Word:
1. sentence in which word is found.
2. dictionary/glossary definition
3. my definition
4. my original sentence using the word

c. Concept of Definition (Word Map) (Schwartz & Raphael, 1985)
A map uses three essential questions: What is it? (Category) What is it like? (Properties) and What are some examples? (Illustrations). This approach expands students' concept of definition beyond that found in the dictionary.

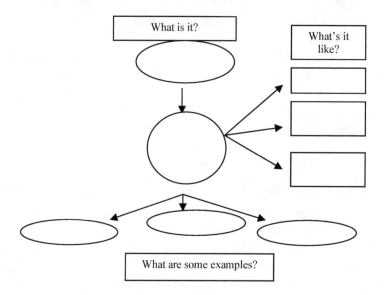

Students can develop a Concept of Definition Map for key concepts and maintain them in a vocabulary notebook. Maps can be developed individually, in pairs, or in small groups followed by a class sharing and discussion.

d. Vocabulary Map (Santa, Havens, & Valdes,2004)
A variation on the Word Map is the vocabulary map where students record definition, a sentence, synonym and a picture.

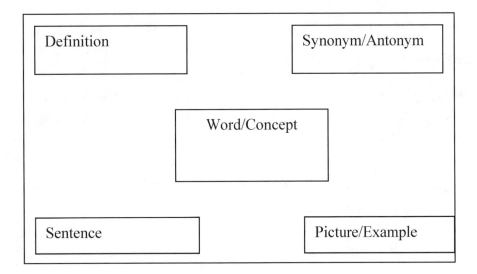

e.   Preview in context

To use this strategy, you would guide the students to locate selected words in the text reading to determine their meaning through context. Here are the steps:

- Select the words to be taught and identify the passages that contain the words.
- Taking each word individually, read the sentence(s) that contains the word.
- Ask students what they think the word means.
- Expand their word meaning by discussing synonyms, antonyms or other meanings of the word.
- After teaching the words, students write the words in their notebooks in an original sentence.

2.   **Vocabulary Reinforcement Methods**

a. Word combining (Santa, Havens, & Valdes, 2004)

In word combining, students form an original sentence or short paragraph using the new vocabulary words. This is an excellent bellwork activity.

-List three to five words on the board or overhead.
-Direct students to write one or two sentences that use all the words.
-Have students share their sentences.

b.   Word puzzles

Word searches, crossword puzzles, bingo, and other board games using the terms and their definitions can reinforce vocabulary. Students can be encouraged to develop their own word puzzles and share them with their peers.

c. Writing activities

Key Words and Summary Sentence (Keogh, 2005)
Display the key words you want them to use and have them write a summary sentence using the words. They may use any form of the key words and arrange them in any order. Young children may draw a picture and write the words to correspond to the illustration.

You can incorporate sentence frames to help students write their summaries:
A ____ is a kind of ____ that…
____ and ____ are similar/different because they …
____ starts with …, then…, and ends with…
____ wanted…, but…, so
____ occurs because…, or ____ causes…. and as a result…

Daily Response Journals

The Daily Response Journal may be conducted with the whole class, small groups, pairs, or individuals. You should hold a short discussion using the vocabulary words and you might provide students with a graphic organizer. Then give students a prompt or a choice of prompts and allow 10 minutes for writing. Sample prompts include:
The most important thing I learned was…
I'm still confused about…
This is important because…

Encourage students to use their vocabulary words in their writing and have them share their responses with the class, small group, or with a peer. You should also collect journals frequently and don't forget to write a reaction.

d. KWL

If you complete the Learning column at periodic points or at the end of a unit, you can also incorporate writing in the activity. Have students transform the information on the KWL chart into a summary or a concept map.

Activity

8.2 Locate the textbook or curriculum guide you will be using. Develop a list of vocabulary terms and design a method to teach and reinforce the words with your students.

3. Extending Word Meaning Methods

a. Morphemic Analysis

Morphemic Analysis is a strategy in which the meanings of words can be determined or inferred by examining their meaningful parts (i.e., prefixes, suffixes, roots, etc.). Research suggests that when students can draw on the structural aspects of an unknown word to determine its meaning, they increase their comprehension. (Scott & Nagy, 1994, Wysocki & Jenkins, 1987).

Morphemes can stand on their own, such as *car* and *bear*. They also can be word parts that have meaning but change or extend the meaning of words when they are added to other morphemes, such as bi-, -un-, -less, or –er. Teaching students the suffix –ology as meaning "the study of" helps them when they encounter words such as geneology, biology, and sociology.

A warning here: Teaching students lists of prefixes, suffixes, and roots is not of value. You need to introduce these morphemes in the context of what they are studying and reading. Unfortunately, there isn't any agreement on how to teach morphemes or on which morphemes to introduce. But, here's an example of how you might introduce a morpheme to your students (Templeton & Pikulski,1999):

The teacher writes the following words on the board and asks: *Do these words have anything in common?* Hopefully, a student will comment that they all end in "er."

Baker	Boxer
Teacher	Player
Lawyer	Manager
Writer	Driver

The teacher then explains that the suffix "er" means "one who" and adding it to a word indicates a person who performs that task (one who bakes, teaches, practices law).

Next, the students work in small groups or pairs to develop additional words that use the "er" suffix. Finally, the teacher introduces the word from the unit/reading (forecaster) and asks students to determine its meaning.

While this example is basic and elementary, the strategy can be applied to all morphemic units.

b. Word sorts

Another technique for extending and reinforcing word meaning is through word sorts. Word sorting is categorizing. When students sort words into categories they are actively analyzing, comparing and contrasting. Bear, et. al (2004) recommend word sorts for every level of learner. While there are many types of sorts focusing on word patterns and sounds, when you want students to focus on meaning, you may want to start by giving students the categories and allowing them to sort the vocabulary words (closed sort). As students understand the process, you can present the words and have the students determine the categories (open sort).

For example, in math students are given the following written on 3x5 cards: ¼, ½, ¾, .25, .50, .75, 1, 5, 10, *fraction, decimal, whole number*

Students work in pairs to sort the cards into meaningful categories.

Here's another example from a high school history course.

Students are given the following terms and asked to sort and form categories:

militarism, peonage, propaganda, reparations, atrocity, mobilize, indigenous ,pacifism, exploit, ultimatum, proletariat, armistice, nationalize, apartheid, appeasement, sanction, containment, fundamentalism, abdicate, homogeneous, heterogeneous, interdependence, repudiate

Students share their sorts and explain their reasoning.

Activity

8.3 Examine your curriculum or a unit you will be teaching. Create a lesson that incorporates morphemic analysis or word sorts or both.

Time for Actual Reading and Writing

Research by Anderson, et. al (1985) concluded that the amount of time students spent in school engaged in independent reading was related to gains in reading achievement. Independent reading time has long been held as an essential in developing reading proficiency; however, reading time in this context is not defined as the use of worksheets or skill sheets. What students need is ample time for actual text reading. Research does not give us suggestions on how much time we should allocate, but Fielding and Pearson (1994) recommend that the time for actual classroom reading should be more than that which is given to learning about reading or talking/writing about what was read.

Independent reading in the classroom should be viewed as practice. All professional athletes, musicians, dancers had to practice many hours to get to their level of proficiency and continue to practice to maintain or develop their ability. So it is with the academic areas,

> Teaching comprehension, unlike assessing comprehension, involves teaching behaviors such as modeling, explaining, thinking aloud, demonstrating, and defining. Teachers must not assume they are teaching children to comprehend text when they mention or assign comprehension skill practice sheets. – D. R. Reutzel & R. B. Cooter, Jr.

such as reading. The more children read, the better they get at it. In addition, they acquire new knowledge and vocabulary which, in turn, increases their reading comprehension.

As many teachers have found, simply saying, *Read chapter 5* may not be effective in getting students to read independently. Some teachers assign independent reading for homework with the idea that they can preserve their classroom time for "teaching" or other activities. Unfortunately, students don't always do their reading homework.

There are some strategies that you can use to enhance students' independent reading time and also ensure that students get the most out of their reading assignments. Two of the best teaching strategies are the Directed Reading Activity and the Directed Reading-Thinking Activity which, when used correctly, can successfully guide your students as they read independently to higher levels of comprehension.

Directed Reading Activity (DRA)

The DRA, introduced by Betts in 1946, has been around a long time and is easily adaptable with all types of reading material. DRA (Betts, 1969) is a strategy that provides students with instructional support before, during, and after reading. The teacher takes an active role as he or she prepares students to read the text by preteaching important vocabulary, eliciting prior knowledge, and providing a purpose for reading.

There are five phases: Readiness, Silent Reading, Comprehension Check and Discussion, Rereading, and Follow-up activities.

1. Readiness – As the term implies, you must first get your students ready to read. We can all agree that stating, *Read the first paragraph, please,* or *Read silently the first section on page 79* are not effective readiness strategies. We develop a student's readiness for reading by doing one or more of the following:

   a. Develop prior knowledge (discussed previously)
      If students do not have the concept(s) needed for the reading, you will need to develop those concepts. You will also help students connect what they already know with the reading through discussion, videos, pictures, etc. If students do not have the necessary concepts, you will need to develop them through direct teaching, demonstrations, Internet activities, etc.

   b. Introduce new vocabulary
      You will need to introduce new vocabulary in context, both orally and visually. This type of introduction is not lengthy and is designed to give students familiarity with the pronunciation and meaning of the words they will meet in the reading. Generally, no more than six words are introduced at a time.

   c. Establish purpose for reading

> Reading without a clear idea of purpose can lead to frustration for students, who may not achieve the results their teachers expect, and to exasperation for teachers, who often fail to understand how their students' comprehension can be so inadequate. – M. C. McKenna & R. D. Robinson

This is perhaps the most crucial readiness activity. Students should know *why* they are reading the material (beside that you told them to do so). If you ask yourself the question, *Why are students reading this?* then you can relate that information to your students. For example, *Read this section to find out the causes of _____;* or *As you read this page, think about the character's feelings;* or *When you read, think about examples of solutions and mixtures in your daily life.* If you don't do anything else to prepare your students, you must give them a purpose to read.

d. Create interest
   When we read material we're interested in, we usually have better comprehension. It's your job to arouse students' interest. Sometimes, just by connecting students' prior knowledge or establishing a purpose, you can generate interest. For example, using KWL allows you to connect to prior learning, develop student generated questions for reading purpose, and create interest in the reading.

The readiness stage should only take ten to fifteen minutes. If your students have absolutely no background knowledge, the readiness stage may take longer, but it should never be overlooked.

2. Silent Reading

In this phase, students read silently the assigned material. With long selections, you should break up the reading into more manageable sections or pages. Students should not read for longer than 20 minutes in order for you to incorporate time to discuss the reading and check comprehension.

While silent reading should be emphasized, you can incorporate other strategies such as buddy reading, tape recordings, or teacher read alouds. You might give a time frame for this phase such as, *You have 15 minutes to read this section.* Two particularly effective organizational strategies for reading include the following:

Read and Say Something

In this strategy, students are given an opportunity to construct meaning and work with a partner. You should provide a chart or transparency with conversation starters. Here's how it works:
- Assign students a partner
- Students read an assigned portion of the selection
- When they are finished, they turn to their partner and "say something" about what they just read. Things to say include:

make a prediction, ask a question, clarify, make a comment or make a connection. It's best to give sentence starters such as, *I predict that… Why did… This is confusing because… This is really saying… This reminds me of…*

- You assign more text to read and the process is repeated.
- After the selection is completed, conduct a whole-class discussion on the reading.

Reading Teams

Students are assigned to a team of 3 or 4 students and take turns reading the selection aloud to their team. It is advised that you structure the reading by telling students how many lines/paragraphs each person is to read aloud.

You can heighten the cooperative nature of this strategy by assigning roles to the members, such as, Team Leader (makes sure everyone reads their section), Task Manager (ensures everyone is on task), Discussion Leader (reads teacher-prepared questions or develops questions with the group), and Checker (makes sure everyone in the group understood the reading material or that they all completed the follow-up activity(ies).

3. Comprehension Check and Discussion

This comprehension check should consist of 3-5 prepared questions on the material read and should include a question on the purpose set for reading. These questions usually focus on the literal and inferential levels and are designed for you to monitor students' comprehension of the material.

After the comprehension check, begin the cycle again. *In this next section, we will read about _____. I want you to read to find out…*

You should establish a reading cycle of Readiness → Silent Reading → Comprehension Check for each section students will be reading.

4. Rereading

After the reading is complete, you can incorporate oral rereading with the comprehension check. For example, students might be directed to: *Read the section that tells you…* as they answer questions, or *Read the part that supports your conclusion.* If students seem confused about a topic or concept, you can direct their rereading to a particular section for clarity (*Let's read the first paragraph on page 90 to understand what we were talking about.*)

5. Follow-up Activities

We're all familiar with a Q&A after reading where the teacher asks a question, calls on one or two students, makes a comment and then asks another question. We also probably remember the teacher who handed out a list of questions (or made students copy them from the overhead) and, then, students answered the questions in writing from the reading followed by a test on Friday. These strategies don't necessarily help foster comprehension. Here are some more productive methods to use as a follow-up to the reading:

a. Reading guides

A reading guide is a written guide that helps students focus on the important concepts in the reading. The guide has also been shown to enhance reading by making it more active, encouraging students to interact with text, and adding the tactile learning style. In addition, guides foster the reading-writing connection and serve as a useful study tool for review. Lastly, guides help reading comprehension. (McKenna & Robinson, 2009)

Guides take many forms. As you develop a guide for your students you need to ask two essential questions:
1. What is the purpose of the reading?
2. What is the learning objective?
When you actually write the guide, format it so it's attractive. A list of 20 questions is not an inviting guide so try to keep questions limited to those focusing on key points. Use clip art, borders around print, and different type (italic, bold, etc.) to get students' attention. Help guide students' reading by giving page numbers and subheadings. Below is a sample reading guide for a history passage on the U.S. Western Expansion.

Read the section on the Western Expansion (pp. 125-135) and complete the following:

1. How did <u>Thomas Jefferson</u> encourage the western expansion of the U.S.?

2. What resulted from the **Lewis and Clark** expedition?

3. What was the impact of Mexico ceding its claim to U.S. territories?

4. What were 3 hardships that faced western pioneers in the 1800s?

5. Make a timeline of *significant* events in U.S. western expansion between 1800-1850.

6. Compare and contrast the **geographical** boundaries of the U.S. in 1783 to 1850 on a map. Indicate countries that held land by using different colors.

Activity

8.4 Research the different types of guides and develop a reading guide for a selection you will be teaching.

b. Reading Response Logs

There are many examples of response logs in the literature. One generic model, adapted from Tovani is the following:

<table>
<tr><td colspan="2" align="center">Reading Response Log</td></tr>
<tr><td colspan="2">

Page _____ to page _____

Summary (4-6 sentences). Retell what you read about.

Response (5-8 sentences).

Possible ways to begin a response:
This connects to my life in this way…
I wonder…
_____ is important because…
I don't understand…
I predict that …
My favorite part so far is…
This is confusing because….

Questions in my head as I was reading this:
</td></tr>
</table>

c. Graphic organizers

   Graphic organizers and their impact on student learning were discussed in Module 3. You can use graphic organizers for review, reinforcement, or as a comprehension check. These visual representations are widely available in textbooks, resources materials and on the Internet.

   http://www.eduplace.com/graphicorganizer
   http://www.teachervision.fen.com/graphic-organizer/printable/6293.html
   http://www.graphic.org/goindex.html
   http://freeology.com
   http://www.region15.org/curriculum/graphicorg.html (Includes a Spanish version of the graphic organizers)

d. Completion of KWL
   Students can work independently, in pairs, or small groups to complete the final column of a KWL

e. Cooperative groups
   Cooperative groups can produce many types of products related to the reading:
   > One sentence summary
   > News story, newspaper, or documentary
   > Brochure
   > Poster
   > Concept Map
   > Graphic Organizer
   > Quiz Questions

Here are three examples of cooperative group activities:

Vocabulary Book

Explain that the group's task is to locate and creatively define unfamiliar or interesting words from the reading. When encountering new words, students should be encouraged to look at the context of the surrounding sentences, engage in a group discussion about the new words, draw upon their prior knowledge of the word or topic, and access print (dictionaries and thesaurus) and online resources for supporting definitions.

RAFT

One activity that incorporates extended writing with the reading is RAFT developed by Nancy Vandevanter (Santa, Havens, & Valdes, 2004). RAFT is an acronym for Role, Audience, Format, and Topic and outlines the decisions students must make prior to writing. *Role* refers to the role of the author: Who are you? Are you a slave, a plantation owner, or a northern business owner?
Audience is to whom is this written? Is this written to a soldier, a congressman, or to the President?
Format tells the student the form of the writing: Is it a letter, a speech, a journal entry, or a news story?
Topic tells the writer to plead, convince, clarify, describe, or complain.

Students might take the viewpoint of an endangered animal pleading with humans in a letter to the editor to protect them and their environment. Another example is to relate a fairy tale or story from the viewpoint of another character. Students assume the role of one of the dwarfs in Snow White in order to clarify their role in her poisoning in the form of a court testimony.

Role Playing

Students assume roles to explore situations that involve considering others' ideas. They might, for example, assume the roles of different story/historical characters and have other students interview them. Other role playing possibilities include:

- improvising a scene using the roles they have created
- depicting the key events or incidents in the story/ event
- choral speaking, rapping, or presenting reader's theatre using key ideas from the story/event
- converting a narrative story into a drama
- using mime to communicate key actions, i.e. a blood cell traveling through the human body

Follow-up activities are designed to build and extend skills or concepts or to enrich students' understanding. Some people view this phase as review and use worksheets on vocabulary, comprehension, or skill practice. It is also the opportunity to use creative activities in writing, role playing or drama, or the visual arts. Research and extended reading could involve the Internet, other texts or library materials.

Activity

8.5 Using reading material from your curriculum, create a lesson plan using the Directed Reading Activity. Be sure to indicate how you would carry out each step of the DRA.

The Directed Reading-Thinking Activity

The directed reading-thinking activity (DRTA) was developed by Stauffer (1969). It is a teaching activity that incorporates predicting, summarizing, and evaluating. Combined with oral retelling and summarizing, the technique helps to develop critical thinking. The DRTA is conducted best using a storybook or picture book with a strong plot and can be adapted for use with expository text using different questioning techniques. (Mariotti & Homan, 2005; Tierney & Readence, 2004)

Step I

To begin the DRTA show the students the cover of the book and read the title. Next, encourage student thinking by asking: *"What do you think this is going to be about? What makes you think that?"* (With expository material, read the chapter title and subheadings, examine any graphic aids, and ask: *"What words do you think will be in the passage? Why do you think that? What do you think this passage is about? What questions do you think will be answered in the reading? Why do you think that?"* All students' responses are accepted and written so students can see them.

> Reading is to the mind what exercise is to the body.
> -Joseph Addison

Step II

In this step, students read silently to a predetermined stopping point. When you reach the stopping point you will ask students to examine the accuracy of their predictions. Ask the students: *"What has happened so far? Which of our predictions were correct? Why? Can we eliminate any predictions? Can we make new predictions?"* (With informational text, ask *"How accurate were our predictions? Prove it. Can we add any new questions?"*)

The reading continues with the predict-read-prove cycle. It seems best to keep the number of stops to a maximum of six as more than six stopping points interrupt the flow of the reading. With long selections, you can use the DRTA with the first half and then switch to the Directed Reading Activity for the second half.

Step III

Once the story or selection is completed, ask students to retell or summarize the reading in their own words.   You can use follow-up activities suggested in your teacher's edition or any of the ideas presented previously with the DRA follow-up.

Activity

8.6 Locate reading material you might use with your students. Create a lesson using the DRTA indicating how you would introduce the lesson and the stopping points.

Time for Student Talk

If we really want students to discuss their reading, then we can't just say to students, *Go talk about your reading.* And the traditional Q&A with the teacher asking all the questions is not the type of discussion we're after either. What we're looking for here is a natural type of conversation. Think about this: When we discuss a movie or TV program with our friends, there isn't a person in the group who has a list of questions for us to answer. If you listen in on these conversations, you will hear phrases such as, *I liked the part when... I thought the ending...Did you see when...*   When we talk about documentaries, we use phrases such as, *I thought it was interesting when... I didn't know that... That part about _____ was fascinating because...*

In the classroom, if you want your students to truly discuss their reading, you must see

yourself as a member of the group rather than as the director. In this sense, you are not the inquisitor but an equal member who is interested in discussing ideas, hypotheses, problems and strategies. Questions are usually open-ended with multiple answers that go beyond a single word or sentence.

What's the author's message? What's important to know? How does this relate to us today? Why should we be concerned with this? How do you see this working in your daily life?

Whether you want students to discuss their reading in small groups or as a whole class, they will need direction on what to talk about or their conversation will <u>not</u> be academically focused. In addition, they will need to have some group discussion "rules" and these rules should be taught, posted, and reviewed.

To begin, you will need to clearly explain to your students the task and outcome of the discussion. For example, *When you're done with this discussion, you will complete... or At the end of the discussion, you will write in your journal….* It is helpful if you develop a group product wherein the students summarize the results of the discussion.

To foster discussion, students should come prepared beyond just reading the assignment. You can:

1. provide a list of conversation starters for them to complete prior to the group work:
    a. I wonder…
    b. I think…
    c. I didn't understand…
    d. I wish…
    e. I liked…
2. provide a brief list of high-order questions from Bloom's application, analysis, synthesis, and evaluation levels for students to work on before they come together as a group. (Questions at Bloom's knowledge and comprehension levels do not necessarily foster a discussion.)
3. have students find and write 3-5 quotes they found interesting and explain why. In group, they share and discuss the quotes.

Quote and page number	Your Comment

4. have students write in reading logs

A reading log can take many forms. Here's an example:

Assigned Reading:
Purpose of Reading
Key Vocabulary Terms
Key Ideas from the Reading
Summary of My Reading
Questions I Still Have

There are several web sites which offer free downloads of reading logs. You should visit some of these sites as you plan how you want your students to record their reading activities.

http://www.countryclipart.com/ReadingLogs/readinglogs.htm
http://edhelper.com/teachers/reading_log.htm
http://www.abcteach.com/directory/basics/reading/reading_logs
http://freeology.com

You can also provide prompts for students to help them write a response in their logs. Prompts can be given as bellwork or homework and help guide the reader into more meaningful responses. Students' responses to such prompts then form the basis of the initial group discussion.

Tell about the reading
Describe the (characters, procedure, discovery, etc)
What's is your opinion of.... Why do you hold that opinion?
Compare _____ with _____.
This is important because…
What does the author mean when he writes…
What are the characteristics of…

Activity

8.7 Create a reading log form to use with your students.

What if students do not come prepared to discuss or were absent when the assignment was given? Provide a quiet space in the classroom for these students to complete their reading and pre-discussion assignment individually before they join the discussion.

Direct Instruction in Reading Skills

Effective teachers routinely offer direct, precise demonstrations of useful reading strategies and model the thinking processes that skilled readers use. These teachers did not say "Watch me" and then assign a worksheet to practice. Rather, effective teachers used a direct instruction approach that includes using think-alouds as they explicitly model the strategy and then provide opportunities for students to practice the strategy with teacher support. (Allington, 2002)

The reading comprehension strategies you teach may be already selected in your curriculum. If not, you can select from those listed below. These strategies must be taught thoroughly as students develop the ability to read more complex text:

- Comparison/contrast
- Cause and effect
- Sequencing
- Main idea and supporting details
- Character analysis
- Literary elements (characters, plot, climax, resolution, etc.)
- Point of view
- Text Structure
- Reading graphic aids
- Inferencing
- Drawing Conclusions
- Predicting/Hypothesizing

> Teaching strategies for the sake of teaching strategies isn't the goal…The only reason to teach kids how to be strategic readers is to help them become more thoughtful about their reading. – Cris Tovani

Direct instruction is a systematic method that has been widely researched and found related to improved student learning (Woolfolk, 2004) The outline that follows is generally referred to as the Madeline Hunter Method and works well for the teaching of any skill.

📖 Introduction/Anticipatory Set

In the introduction to the lesson, you should present the lesson objective, the reason for learning the skill, when to use the skill, and how the skill can help them. (*This will improve your reading comprehension; This is on the state reading test,* etc.) You can also provide the "hook" to grab students' attention.

📖 Teaching/Presentation

You must present the strategy/skill in simple terms and take students through several demonstrations in which you model the steps of the strategy/skill. Here, you will use think-alouds to share how you mentally approach the task. After a few demonstrations, you should elicit student responses in a structured manner. Present a new task and ask, *What do I do first, What should I look for?, How do I figure out what to do next, What are the key words that signal what I should do?*

📖 Guided Practice

During this phase, students work through an activity or exercise under your direct supervision. You move around the room and ensure that students are correctly applying the skill/strategy. If a student is having difficulty, you would give immediate remediation. When students are able to use the strategy or skill correctly at least 70% of the time, then they are ready for independent work. Close this portion of the lesson by reviewing the key points of the lesson.

📖 Independent Practice

Independent practice is considered reinforcement practice. This may be seatwork or homework but you will need to continue monitoring student performance and giving feedback and encouragement as needed.

Direct Instruction Lesson Example

Objective: Students will complete a comparison-contrast Venn diagram on two objects.

Introduction

1. Hold up two different spoons for students to focus on as they explore the meaning of the terms *compare* and *contrast. Say: How are these alike?*
2. Write on the board (or overhead) students' responses.
3. Create a new column and ask: *How are these different?*
4. Based on the information in the lists, lead a class discussion on the definitions of the words *compare* and *contrast.* Refer to examples on the board to clarify the difference between the two terms.
5. Explain that understanding how two or three things are alike and different is a valuable strategy for categorizing and that using this skill can help them in their reading of the textbook. Then, as a class, brainstorm ways that they use compare and contrast in their daily life.

Teaching Presentation

Show a picture of a bird and a fish. Demonstrate with a think-aloud, how you look for similarities and differences and complete a Venn diagram while doing so.

Guided Practice

1. Present two new pictures. Ask pairs of students to complete a Venn diagram. Circulate and assist.
2. Ask students to share their responses and write them in a Venn diagram on the overhead.
3. Review the key points of comparison-contrast.

Independent Practice

1. Give students two new pictures and have each complete a Venn diagram independently.
2. Have pairs share their completed diagrams.

Periodic Review & Application

Subsequent lessons should focus comparing characters in a story, historical events, countries, etc., and on the key words they would encounter in their reading which signal a comparison-contrast structure.

Activity

8.8 Examine your content and determine a reading skill from the list above that would support your students' comprehension. Develop a direct instruction lesson for that skill.

Planning for Reading

It's a good idea to examine the reading assignment, analyze it, and anticipate what might cause students problems. Here's a planning guide, adapted from Tovani (2004), to help you:

1. What is the objective of the lesson? What will students be expected to know and/or do as a result of the reading?
2. What will students be expected to do with the material they are reading? (take notes, solve problems, complete study guide, etc.)
3. What might be problem areas for students?
    a. vocabulary/concepts
    b. text structure
    c. background knowledge
4. What reading skill(s) should I model or reinforce?

A Supportive Environment

If you want your students to comprehend what they read and hear, you will need to provide a classroom environment that supports and encourages comprehension. More importantly, we have to stop thinking of reading instruction as that which occurs only in the primary or intermediate elementary years and only in reading classes.

What students read may be changing. Students might now see their textbooks in the form of a CD and may also access the text through a publisher website. Many experts point out that the textbook will be an outmoded artifact as the computer becomes a major teaching tool. Reading comprehension and thinking skills, whether used with a paper-bound text or on a computer screen,

> **A** wonderful thing about a book, in contrast to a computer screen, is that you can take it to bed with you.   - Daniel J. Boorstin

are still the same skills. In fact, the ability to discriminate relevant information from the irrelevant is even more critical with students' use of the Internet. So, whether you use the paper version or the flat screen, one of your major tasks will be to support your students' reading comprehension by incorporating the five aspects described here.

References

Academic Leadership. (2007). Providing students with effective feedback. http://www.academicleadership.org/leader_action_tips/Providing_Students_with_E ffective_Feedback.

Adams, M., & Bertram, B. (1980). *Background Knowledge and Reading Comprehension* (Reading Ed. Rep. No. 13). Urbana: University of Illinois Press, Center for the Study of Reading. (ERIC Document Reproduction Service ED 181 431)

Alderman, T. W. (1997). *Discipline: A Total Approach Resource Book.* Beaufort, SC: Resources for Professionals.

Albert, L. (1989). *A Teacher's Guide to Cooperative Discipline: How to Manage Your Classroom and Promote Self-Esteem.* Minn.: AGS.

Allington, R. L. (2001). *What really matters for struggling readers: Designing research-based programs.* New York: Addison-Wesley Longman.

Allington, R. (2002). What I've learned about effective reading instruction from a decade of studying exemplary elementary classroom teachers. *Phi Delta Kappan, 83,* 740-747.

Anderson, R. C., Hiebert, E. H., Scott, J. A., & Wilkinson, I.A.G. (1985). *Becoming a Nation of Readers.* Washington, D. C.: National Institute of Education.

Anderson, R. C., Reynolds, R. E., Schallert, D. L., & Goetz, E. T. (1977). Frameworks for comprehending discourse. *American Educational Research Journal, 14,* 367-382.

Airasian, P. & Russell, M. (2007). *Classroom Assessment: Concepts and Applications, 6th ed.* New York: McGraw-Hill.

Bangert-Downs, R. L., Kulik, C. C., Kulik, J. A., & Morgan, M. (1991). The instructional effects of feedback in test-like events. Review of Educational Research, 61(2), 213-238. Bank Street Learning Six Domains of Teaching. http://www.bankstreet.edu/tne/domains.html

Barger, G. W. (1983). Classroom testing procedures and student anxiety. *Improving College and University Teaching, 31* (1), 25-26.

Betts, E. A. (1969). *Foundations of Reading Instruction.* NY: American Book Co.

Bloom, B. S., Englehart, M. B., Furst, E. J., Hill, W. H., & Krathwohl, O.R. (1956). *Taxonomy of Educational objectives: The Classification of Educational Goals. Handbook 1: The Cognitive Domain.* New York: Longman.

Bonwell, C. & Eison, J. (1991). *Active Learning: Creating Excitement in the Classroom.* Washington, D.C.: ASHE-ERIC.

Borich, G. (2006). *Effective Teaching Methods: Research Based Practice,* 6th ed. New York: Prentice Hall.

Buckley, P. K, & Cooper, J. M. (1978). *An ethnographic study of an elementary school teacher's establishment and maintenance of group norms.* Paper presented at the annual meeting of the American Education Research Association, Toronto, Canada.

Burden, P. R. & Byrd, D. M. (2007). *Methods for Effective Teaching: Meeting the Needs of All Students,* 4th ed. Boston: Allyn and Bacon.

Canter, L. & Canter, M. (2001). *Assertive Discipline: Positive Behavior Management for Today's Classroom, 3rd ed.* Bloomington, IN: Solution Tree.

Christen, W. L. & Murphy, T. J. (1991). Increasing comprehension by activating prior knowledge. ERIC Digest. ERIC Document Reproduction Service ED328885

Clark, C. M. & Yinger, R. (1988). Teacher planning. In D. Berliner and B. Rosenshine (Eds.), *Talks to Teachers,* pp. 342-365. New York: Random House.

Cooper, H. (1989). Synthesis of research on homework. *Educational Leadership, 47*(3), 85-91.

Cooper, J.D. & Kiger, N.D. (2003). *Literacy: Helping children construct meaning,* 5th ed. Boston: Houghton Mifflin Company.

Cooper, T. L. (no date). The benefits of progress monitoring our students. http://www.teachernetwork.org/NTNY/nyhelp/Professional_Development/program. htm.

Cotton, K. (1988). Monitoring student learning in the classroom. School Improvement Research Series Close-Up #4. Portland: OR: Northwest Regional Education Lab. ED 298085. http://www.nwrel.org/scpd/sirs/2/cu4.html.

Crane, S. (no date). Levels of feedback. http://coe.sdsu.edu/eet/Articles/lofeedback/start.htm.

Cunningham, P. M. & Allington, R. L. (2007). *Classroom that Work: They Can All Read and Write, 4th ed.* NY: Longman.

Dale, E. (1969). *Audio-Visual Methods in Teaching,* 3rd ed. Austin, TX: Holt, Rinehart & Winston.

Davey, B. (1983). Think-aloud: Modeling the cognitive processes of reading comprehension. *Journal of Reading, 27,* 44-47.

Doolan, L. S., & Honigsfeld, A. (2000). Illuminating the new standards with learning style: Striking a perfect match. *Clearing House, 73*(5), 274-278.

Dreikurs, R., Cassel, P. & Ferguson-Dreikurs, E. (2005). *Discipline without Tears: How to Reduce Conflict and Establish Cooperation in the Classroom.* NJ: Wiley.

Dunn, E. W. (2001). Do seating arrangements and assignments = classroom management? http://www.education-world.com/a_curr/curr330.shtml.

Dweck, C. S. (1975). The role of expectations in the alleviation of learned helplessness. *Journal of Personality and Social Psychology, 11,* 674-685.

Elawar, M. C., & Corno, L. (1985). A factorial experiment in teachers' written feedback on student homework: Changing teacher behavior a little rather than a lot. *Journal of Educational Psychology, 77,* 162-173.

Fielding, L. G. & Pearson, P. D. (1994). Synthesis of Research: Reading comprehension-What works. *Educational Leadership, 51*(5). http://www.ascd.org/video.guides/reading02/resources/reading2_p.html

Glasser, W. (1986). *Control Theory in the Classroom.* New York: Harper and Row.

Gillet, J., Temple, C., Crawford, A., & Cooney, B. (2007). *Understanding Reading Problems: Assessment and Instruction,* 7th ed. Boston: Pearson/Allyn and Bacon.

Hanf, M. B. (1971). Mapping: A technique for translating reading into thinking. *Journal of Reading, 13,* 225-230.

Hunter, M., & Barker, G. (1989). If at first…: Attribution theory in the classroom. *Annual Edition: Educational Psychology, 89/90.* Guilford, CT: Duskin.

Johnson, D. W., Johnson, R. T., & Holubec, E. J. (1988). *Advanced Cooperative Learning.* Edina, Minn.: Interaction Book Company.

Jones, V. & Jones, L. (2010). *Comprehensive Classroom Management: Creating Communities of Support and Solving Problems.* NJ: Merrill.

Kagan, S. (1999). *Cooperative Learning.* San Clemente, CA: Kagan.

Keogh, V. K. (2005). Key Words: Writing Summary Sentences. In Thompkins, G. E. & Blanchfield, C. *50 Ways to Develop Strategic Writers*, pp. 69-71, NJ: Pearson/Allyn & Bacon.

Kirkland, M.C. (1971). The effects of tests on students and schools. *Review of Educational Research, 41,* 303-351.

Kizlik, R. (2005). *Classroom Management, Management of Student Conduct, Effective Praise Guidelines, and a Few Things to Know About ESOL Thrown in for Good Measure.* Retrieved November 12, 2005, from http://www.adprima.com/Printer/printmanaging.htm

Kluth, P. (2005). Differentiating instruction: 5 easy strategies for inclusive classrooms. http://www.paulaKluth.com/articles/diffstrategies.html.

Lysakowski, R. S., & Walberg, H. J. (1981). Classroom reinforcement and learning: A quantitative synthesis. *Journal of Educational Research, 75,* 69-77.

Mariotti, A. P. & Homan, S. P. (2005). *Linking Reading Assessment to Instruction: An Application Worktext for Elementary Classroom Teachers,* 4th ed. NJ: Lawrence Erlbaum Asso.,

Marzano, R., Marzano, J., & Pickering, D. (2003). *Classroom Management that Works: Research-Based Strategies for Every Teacher.* Alexandria, VA: ASCD.

Marzano, R., Pickering, D., & Pollock, J. (2001*). Classroom Instruction the Works: Research-Based Strategies for Increasing Student Achievement.* Alexandria, VA: ASCD.

Maslow, A. H. (1968*). Toward a Psychology of Being,* 2nd ed. New York: Van Nostrand Reinhold.

McKenna, M. C. & Robinson, R. D. (2009). *Teaching through Text: Reading and Writing in the Content Areas.* Boston: Pearson/Allyn & Bacon.

Moore, R. T. & Davies, J. A. (1984). Predicting GED scores on the basis of expectancy, valence, intelligence and pretest skill levels with the disadvantaged. *Educational and Psychological Measurement, 44,* 483-490.

Myers-Walls, Judith A. (2004). *Finding the Causes of Misbehavior.* Retrieved October 30, 2005 from http://www.ces.purdue.edu/providerparent/PDF%20Links/FindingCausesMisbehavior.pdf

Ogle, D. M. (1986). K-W-L: A teaching model that develops active reading of expository text. *The Reading Teacher, 39*: 564-570.

Performance Learning Systems (2007). The Benefits of Multisensory Teaching and Sensory Words. http://www.plsweb.com/resources/newsletters/emews_archives/63/2007/05/07.

Popham, W. J. (2005). *Classroom Assessment: What Teachers Need to Know*, 4th ed. Boston: Pearson/ Allyn and Bacon.

Pressley, M. (2000). Comprehension instruction: What makes sense now, what might make sense soon. *Handbook of Reading Research: Volume III* by Kamil, Mosenthal, Pearson, and Barr. http://www.readingonline.org/articles/handbook/pressley/index.html

Ramsden, A. (1999). Seating arrangement. http://www.uwsp.edu/Education/pshaw/Seating%20Arrangements.htm.

Reutzel, D. R., & Cooter, R. B. (2005). *The essentials of teaching children to read: What every teacher needs to know.* NJ: Pearson/Merrill/Prentice Hall.

Rose, M. R. (2001). Reading comprehension: What works? http//:www.learnnc.org/1p/pages779?style=print.

Rummelhart, D. E. (1980). Schemata: The building blocks of cognition. In, *Theoretical Issues in Reading Comprehension*. Ed. Rand J. Spiro. Hillsdale, NJ: Erlbaum.

Rutherford, P. (2002). *Instruction for All Students.* Alexandria, VA: Just ASK Publications

Santa, C., Havens, L., & Valdes, B. (2004). *Project CRISS*, 3rd ed. Dubuque, IO: Kendell-Hunt.

Schwartz, R. M. & Raphael, T. E. (1985). Concepts of definition: A key to improving students' vocabulary. *The Reading Teacher, 39* (2), 198-205.

Scott, J. A., & Nagy, W. E. (1994). Vocabulary development. In Purves, A. C., Papa, L., & Jordan, S. (Eds.) *Encyclopedia of English Studies and Language Arts, Vol. 2.* New York: Scholastic.

Shavelson, R. J. (1987). Planning. In M. Dunkin (Ed.), *The International Encyclopedia of Teaching and Teacher Education*, pp. 483-486. New York: Pergamon Press.

Shearer, A. P. (1997). *The Culturally Responsive Classroom: Building a Climate of Success for All Students.* Paper presented at the Kappa Delta Pi Urban Education Conference, Tampa, Fl.

Short, K.G., Harste, J., & Burke, C. (1996). *Creating Classrooms for Authors and Inquirers,* 2nd ed. Portsmouth, NH: Heinemann.

Silverman, H. & Shearer, A. (1985*). Using Questioning Techniques: FPMS Learning Package 5.* Tallahassee, Fl: Florida State Department of Education.

Stahl, S. A. (1999). *Vocabulary development: From research to practice* (Vol. 2). Cambridge, MA: Brookline Books.

Stahl, S. A. & Vancel, S. J. (1986). Discussion is what makes semantic maps work in vocabulary instruction. *The Reading Teacher, 40,* 62-67.

Stauffer, R. (1969). *Directing reading maturity as a cognitive process.* NY: Harper & Row.

Stiggins, R. (1997). *Student-Centered Classroom Assessment,* 2nd ed. Columbus, Ohio: Merrill.

Styles, D. (2001). *Class Meetings: Building Leadership, Problem-Solving and Decision-Making Skills in the Respectful Classroom.* Portland, ME: Stenhouse Publ.

Szafran, R. F. (1981). Question-pool study guides: Effects on test anxiety and learning retention. *Teacher Sociology, 9,* 31-43.

Tompkins, G. E. & Blanchfield, C. (2005). *50 Ways to Develop Strategic Writers.* NJ: Pearson.

Templeton, S. & Pikulski, J. (1999). Building the foundations of literacy: The importance of vocabulary and spelling development. http://www.eduplace.com/rdg/hmsv/expert/research.html.

Thiagarajan, S. (2005). *Thiagi's Interactive Lectures.* Alexandria, VA: ASTD Press.

Tierney, R. J., & Readence, J. E. (2004). *Reading Strategies and Practices: A Compendium,* 6th ed. Boston: Allyn and Bacon

Tomlinson, C. A. (2000).*The Differentiated Classroom: Responding to the Needs of All Learners.* Alexandria, VA: ASCD.

Tompkins, G. E. (1998). *50 Literacy Strategies, Step by Step.* NJ: Merrill/Prentice Hall.

Tovani, C. (2004). *Do I Really Have to Teach Reading?* Maine: Stenhouse.

Wagstaff, J. M. (1999). *Teaching Reading and Writing with Word Walls.* New York: Scholastic.

Weiner, B. (1989). *An Attributional Theory of Motivation and Emotion.* New York: Springer.

Wiggins, G., & McTighe, J. (1998). *Understanding By Design.* Alexandria, VA:ASCD.

Wiggins, Grant. (1998). *Educative Assessment: Designing Assessments to Inform and Improve Student Performance*. San Francisco: Jossey-Bass Inc.

Wolfgang, C. H. (2001). *Solving Discipline and Classroom Management Problems: Methods and Models for Today's Teachers.* Roseville, CA: Prima Publishing.

Wong, H. K., & Wong, R. T. (2001). *The First Days of School: How to Be an Effective Teacher.* Mountain View, CA: Harry K. Wong Publications, Inc.

Woolfolk, A. (2004). *Educational Psychology*, 9th ed. Boston: Pearson/Allyn & Bacon.

Wormeli, R. (2005). *Summarization in Any Subject: 50 Techniques to Improve Student Learning.* Alexandria, VA: ASDC.

Wysocki, K., & Jenkins, J. (1987). Deriving word meanings through morphological generalizations. *Reading Research Quarterly, 22,* 66-81.

About the Author

Arleen Mariotti retired from public school service in 2007 after 37 years in education. She received her B.A. and M.Ed. from the University of Florida and her Ph.D. from the University of South Florida. Her areas of expertise include reading assessment and diagnosis, effective teaching, and content area reading. She has served as a classroom teacher, reading specialist, program evaluator, staff development specialist, and college professor. She has created and delivered numerous teacher training programs in reading, writing, cooperative learning, and alternative assessment. She has presented papers at regional and national conferences and served on the Manuscript Review Board for the International Reading Association. She is co-author of *Linking Reading Assessment to Instruction*, 5th ed. and, most recently, serves an adjunct instructor at the University of South Florida, Tampa, Florida.